IN BLACK AND WHITE

AND

UNDER THE DEODARS

By

RUDYARD KIPLING

STANDARD BOOK COMPANY

LONDON   NEW YORK

"Punjab Edition"
ORSAMUS TURNER HARRIS
MCMXXX

PRINTED IN THE
UNITED STATES OF AMERICA

CONTENTS

IN BLACK AND WHITE

UNDER THE DEODARS

IN BLACK AND WHITE

"Smiting himself softly on the breast."

—*On the City Wall, p. 75.*

In Black and White

DEDICATION

To MY MOFT DEARE FATHER,—When I was in your Houfe and we went abroade together, in the outfkirtes of the Citie, among the Gentoo Wreftlours, you had poynted me how in all Empryzes he gooing forth flang backe alwaies a Word to hym that had infruct hym in his Crafte to the better Sneckynge of a Victorie or at the leafte the auoidance of aine great Defeate: And prefentlie each man wolde run to his *Vftad* (which is as we fhoulde fay *Mafter*) and geat fuch as he deferued of Admonefhment, Reprouf and Council, concernynge the Gripp, the Houlde, Crofs-buttock and Fall, and then lay to afrefhe.

In lyke maner I, drawynge back a lytel, from this my Rabble and Encompafment of Labour, have runn afyde to you who were euer my *Vftad* and Speake as it were in your priuie Eare (yet that others may knowe) that if I have here done aught of Faire Crafte and Reverentiall it is come from your hande as trewly (but by i. Degree remouen) as though it had been the coperture of thys Booke that you haue made for me in loue.

3

How may I here tell of that Tender Diligence which in my wauerynge and inconftante visages was in all tymes about me to showe the pafsions and Occafions, Shifts, Humours, and Sports that in due proporcion combinate haue bred that Rare and Terrible Myftery the which, for lacke of a more compleat Venderftandinge, the Worlde has cauled Man: aswel the maner in which you shoulde goo about to pourtraie the same, a lytel at a tyme in Feare and Decencie. By what hand, when I wolde have dabbled a Greene and unvefed Pen in all Earthe Heauen and Hell, bicaufe of the pitiful Confidence of Youthe, was I bounde in and reftrict to wayte tyl I coulde in fome fort difcerne from the Shadowe, that is not by any peynes to be toucht, the small Kernel and Subftance that mighte conforme to the sclendernefs of my Capacitie. All thys and other Council (that, though I dyd then not followe, Tyme hath since fadlie prouen trewe) is my unpayable Debt to you (moft deare Father) and for marke I have set afyde for you, if you will take it, thys my thirde Booke. The more thys and no other fenfe it is of common knowledge that Men do rather efteem a Pebble gathered under the Burn-ynge Lyne (or anie place that they haue gone farr to travel in) than the Paueway of theyr owne Citie, though that may be the better wrought. Your Charitie and the large Tendernefs that I haue nowhere founde fenfe I haue gone from your Houfe shall look upon it fauorably and

ouerpafs the Blemyfhes, Spottes, Foul Crafte,
and Maculations that do as thoroughly marke it
as anie Toil of Me. None the lefs it is fett pre-
fomptuoufly before that Wilde Beafte the Pub-
lick which, though when aparte and one by one
examined is but compoft of such meere Men and
Women as you in theyr outwarde form peynt
and I would fayne peynt in theyr inward work-
ynges, yet in totalitie, is a Great and thanklefse
God (like unto Dagon) upon whofe Altars a man
muft offer of his Befte alone of the Prieftes
(which they caul Reuiewers) pack him emtie
awai. If I faile in thys Seruyce you shall take
me afyde and giue me more inftruction, which
is but the olde Counfel unreguarded and agayne
made playne: As our *Vtads* take hym whofe Nofe
is rubben in the dyrte and speak in hys Eare.
But thys I knowe, that if I fail or if I geat my
Wage from the God aforefayd; and thus dance
perpetually before that Altar till He be wearyed,
the Wifdom that made in my Vfe, when I was
neere to liften, and the Sweep and Swing tem-
perate of the Pen that, when I was afarr, gaue
me alwaies and untyryng the most delectable Till-
age of that Wifdom shall neuer be lackiynge
to me in Lyfe.

And though I am more rich herein than the
richeft, my prefent Pouertie can but make return
in thys lytel Booke which your owne Toil has
nobilitated beyon the deferuynge of the Writer
your Son.

INTRODUCTION

BY KADIR BAKSH, KHITMATGAR

HAZUR,—Through your favor this is a book written by my sahib. I know that he wrote it, because it was his custom to write far into the night; I greatly desiring to go to my house. But there was no order; therefore it was my fate to sit without the door until the work was accomplished. Then came I and made shut all the papers in the office-box, and these papers, by the peculiar operation of Time and owing to the skillful manner in which I picked them up from the floor, became such a book as you now see. God alone knows what is written therein, for I am a poor man and the sahib is my father and my mother, and I have no concern with his writings until he has left his table and gone to bed.

Nabi Baksh, clerk, says that it is a book about the black men—common people. This is a manifest lie, for by what road can my sahib have acquired knowledge of the common people? Have I not, for several years, been perpetually with the sahib; and throughout that time have I not stood between him and the other servants who would persecute him with complaints or vex him with idle tales about my work? Did I not smite Dunnoo, the groom, only yesterday in the matter of the badness of the harness-composition which I had procured? I am the head of the sahib's household and hold his purse. Without me he does not know where are his rupees or his clean collars. So great is my power over the sahib and the love that he bears to me! Have I ever told the sahib about the customs of servants or black men? Am I a fool? I have said "very good talk" upon all occasions. I have always cut smooth his wristbands with scissors, and timely warned him of the passing away of his tobacco that he might not be left smokeless upon a Sunday. More than this I have not done. The sahib can not go out to dinner lacking my aid. How then should he know aught that I did not tell him? Certainly Nabi Baksh is a liar.

None the less this is a book, and the sahib wrote it, for his name is in it, and it is not his washing-book. Now, such is the wisdom of the sahib-log, that, upon opening this thing, they will instantly discover the purport. Yet I would of their favor beg them to observe how correct is the order of the pages, which I have counted, from the first to the last. Thus, One is followed by Two and Two by Three, and so forward to the end of the book. Even as I picked the pages one by one with great trouble from the floor, when the sahib had gone to bed, so have they been placed; and there is not a fault in the whole account. And this is my work. It was a great burden, but I accomplished it; and if the sahib gains honor by that which he has written—and God knows what he is always writing about—I, Kadir Baksh, his servant, also have a claim to honor.

AT HOWLI THANA

His own shoe, his own head.—*Native Proverb*.

As a messenger, if the heart of the Presence be moved to so great favor. And on six rupees. Yes, sahib, for I have three little, little children, whose stomachs are always empty, and corn is now but twenty pounds to the rupee. I will make so clever a messenger that you shall all day long be pleased with me, and, at the end of a year, bestow a turban. I know all the roads of the station and many other things. Aha, sahib! I am clever. Give me service. I was aforetime in the police. A bad character? Now without doubt an enemy has told his tale. Never was I a scamp. I am a man of clean heart, and all my words are true. They knew this when I was in the police. They said: "Afzal Khan is a true speaker in whose words men may trust." I am a Delhi Pathan, sahib—all Delhi Pathans are good men. You have seen Delhi? Yes, it is true that there be many scamps among the Delhi Pathans. How wise is the sahib! Nothing is hid from his eyes, and he will make me messenger, and I will take all his notes secretly and without ostentation. Nay, sahib, God is my witness that I meant no evil. I have long desired to serve

9

under a true sahib—a virtuous sahib. Many
sahibs are as devils unchained. With these sahibs
I would take no service—not though all the
stomachs of my little children were crying for
bread.

Why am I not still in the police? I will speak
true talk. An evil came to the Thana—to Ram
Baksh, the Havildar, and Maula Baksh, and
Juggut Ram and Bhim Singh and Suruj Bul.
Ram Baksh is in the jail for a space, and so also
is Maula Baksh.

It was at the Thana of Howli, on the road that
leads to Gokral-Seetarun, wherein are many
dacoits. We were all brave men—Rustums.
Wherefore we were sent to that Thana which
was eight miles from the next Thana. All day
and all night we watched for dacoits. Why does
the sahib laugh? Nay, I will make a confession.
The dacoits were too clever, and, seeing this,
we made no further trouble. It was in hot
weather. What can a man do in the hot days?
Is the sahib who is so strong—is he, even, vigorous in that hour? We made an arrangement
with the dacoits for the sake of peace. That
was the work of the Havildar, who was fat. Ho!
ho! sahib, he is now getting thin in the jail
among the carpets. The Havildar said: "Give
us no trouble, and we will give you no trouble.
At the end of the reaping send us a man to lead
before the judge, a man of infirm mind against
whom the trumped-up case will break down.

Thus we shall save our honor." To this talk the dacoits agreed, and we had no trouble at the Thana, and could eat melons in peace, sitting upon our charpoys all day long. Sweet as sugar-cane are the melons of Howli.

Now, there was an assistant commissioner— a Stunt Sahib, in that district, called Yunkum Sahib. Aha! He was hard—hard even as is the sahib who, without doubt, will give me the shadow of his protection. Many eyes had Yunkum Sahib, and moved quickly through his district. Men called him The Tiger of Gokral-Seetarun, because he would arrive unannounced and make his kill, and before sunset, would be giving trouble to the Tehsildars thirty miles away. No one knew the comings or goings of Yunkum Sahib. He had no camp, and when his horse was weary he rode upon a devil-carriage. I do not know its name, but the sahib sat in the midst of three silver wheels that made no creaking, and drove them with his legs, prancing like a bean-fed horse—thus. A shadow of a hawk upon the fields was not more without noise than the devil-carriage of Yunkum Sahib. It was here; it was there; it was gone; and the rapport was made, and there was trouble. Ask the Tehsildar of Rohestri how the hen-stealing came to be known, sahib.

It fell upon a night that we of the Thana slept according to custom upon our charpoys, having eaten the evening meal and drunk tobacco.

When we awoke in the morning, behold, of our
six rifles not one remained! Also, the big police-
book that was in the Havildar's charge was gone.
Seeing these things, we were very much afraid,
thinking of our parts that the dacoits, regardless
of honor, had come by night, and put us to shame.
Then said Ram Baksh, the Havildar: "Be silent!
The business is an evil business, but it may yet
go well. Let us make the case complete. Bring
a kid and my tulwar. See you not now, oh fools?
A kick for a horse, but a word is enough for a
man."

We of the Thana, perceiving quickly what was
in the mind of Havildar, and greatly fearing that
the service would be lost, made haste to take the
kid into the inner room, and attended to the words
of the Havildar. "Twenty dacoits came," said
the Havildar, and we, taking his words, repeated
after him according to custom. "There was a
great fight," said the Havildar, "and of us no
man escaped unhurt. The bars of the window
were broken. Suruj Bul, see thou to that; and,
oh, men put speed into your work, for a runner
must get the news to The Tiger of Gokral-
Seetarun." Thereon, Suruj Bul, leaning with
his shoulder, brake in the bars of the window,
and I, beating her with a whip, made the
Havildar's mare skip among the melon-beds till
they were much trodden with hoof-prints.

These things being made, I returned to the
Thana, and the goat was slain; and certain por-

tions of the walls were blackened with fire, and
each man dipped his clothes a little into the blood
of the goat. Know, oh, sahib, that a wound made
by man upon his own body can, by those skilled,
be easily discerned from a wound wrought by
another man. Therefore, the Havildar, taking
his tulwar, smote one of us lightly on the forearm
in the fat, and another on the leg, and a third on
the back of the hand. Thus dealt he with all of
us till the blood came; and Suruj Bul, more eager
than the others, took out much hair. Oh, sahib,
never was so perfect an arrangement. Yea, even
I would have sworn that the Thana had been
treated as we said. There was smoke and breaking and blood and trampled earth.

"Ride now, Maula Baksh," said the Havildar,
"to the house of the Stunt Sahib, and carry the
news of the dacoity. Do you also, oh, Afzal
Khan, run there, and take heed that you are mired
with sweat and dust on your in-coming. The
blood will be dry on the clothes. I will stay and
send a straight report to the Dipty Sahib, and we
will catch certain that ye know of, villagers, so
that all may be ready against the Dipty Sahib's
arrival."

Thus Maula Baksh rode and I ran hanging on
the stirrup, and together we came in an evil plight
before The Tiger of Gokral-Seetarun in the
Rohestri tehsil. Our tale was long and correct,
sahib, for we gave even the names of the dacoits
and the issue of the fight, and besought him to

come. But The Tiger made no sign, and only
smiled after the manner of sahibs when they have
a wickedness in their hearts. "Swear ye to the
rapport?" said he, and we said: "Thy servants
swear. The blood of the fight is but newly dry
upon us. Judge thou if it be the blood of the
servants of the Presence, or not." And he said:
"I see. Ye have done well." But he did not call
for his horse or his devil-carriage, and scour the
land as was his custom. He said: "Rest now
and eat bread, for ye be wearied men. I will
wait the coming of the Dipty Sahib."

Now, it is the order that the Havildar of the
Thana should send a straight report of all
dacoities to the Dipty Sahib. At noon came he,
a fat man and an old, and overbearing withal,
but we of the Thana had no fear of his anger;
dreading more the silences of The Tiger of Gokral-Seetarun. With him came Ram Baksh, the
Havildar, and the others, guarding ten men of
the village of Howli—all men evil affected toward
the police of the Sirkar. As prisoners they came,
the irons upon their hands, crying for mercy—
Imam Baksh, the farmer, who had denied his
wife to the Havildar, and others, ill-conditioned
rascals against whom we of the Thana bore spite.
It was well done, and the Havildar was proud.
But the Dipty Sahib was angry with the Stunt
for lack of zeal, and said "Dam-Dam" after the
custom of the English people, and extolled the
Havildar. Yunkum Sahib lay still in his long

chair. "Have the men sworn?" said Yunkum
Sahib. "Ay, and captured ten evil-doers," said
the Dipty Sahib. "There be more aboard in your
charge. Take horse—ride, and go in the name
of the Sirkar!" "Truly there be more evil-doers
abroad," said Yunkum Sahib, "but there is no
need of a horse. Come all men with me."

I saw the mark of a string on the temple of
Imam Baksh. Does the Presence know the tor-
ture of the Cold Draw? I saw also the face of
The Tiger of Gokral-Seetarun, the evil smile was
upon it, and I stood back ready for what might
befall. Well it was, sahib, that I did this thing.
Yunkum Sahib unlocked the door of his bath-room,
and smiled anew. Within lay the six rifles and
the big police-book of the Thana of Howli! He
had come by night in the devil-carriage that is
noiseless as a ghoul, and moving among us asleep,
had taken away both the guns and the book!
Twice had he come to the Thana, taking each
time three rifles. The liver of the Havildar was
turned to water, and he fell scrabbling in the
dirt about the boots of Yunkum Sahib, crying,
"Have mercy!"

And I? Sahib, I am a Delhi Pathan, and a
young man with little children. The Havildar's
mare was in the compound. I ran to her and
rode; the black wrath of the Sirkar was behind
me, and I knew not wither to go. Till she dropped
and died I rode the red mare; and by the blessing
of God, who is without doubt on the side of all

just men, I escaped. But the Havildar and the rest are now in jail. . . . I am a scamp! It is as the Presence pleases. God will make the Presence a Lord, and give him a rich *Memsahib* as fair as a peri to wife, and many strong sons, if he makes me his orderly. The mercy of Heaven be upon the sahib! Yes, I will only go to the bazaar and bring my children to these so-palace-like quarters, and then—the Presence is my father and my mother, and I, Afzal Khan, am his slave.

Ohe, *Sirdar-ji!* I also am of the household of the sahib.

DRAY WARA YOW DEE

FOR jealousy is the rage of a man; therefore he will not spare it the day of vengeance.
— *Prov.* vii. 34.

ALMONDS and raisins, sahib? Grapes from Cabul? Or a pony of the rarest if the sahib will only come with me. He is thirteen three, sahib, plays polo, goes in a cart, carries a lady and— Holy Kurshed and the Blessed Imams, it is the sahib himself! My heart is made fat and my eye glad. May you never be tired! As is cold water in the Tirah, so is the sight of a friend in a far place. And what do you in this accursed land? South of Delhi, sahib, you know the saying— "Rats are the men and trulls the women." It was an order? Ahoo! An order is an order till one is strong enough to disobey. Oh, my brother, oh, my friend, we have met in an auspicious hour! Is all well in the heart and the body and the house? In a lucky day have we two come together again.

I am to go with you? Your favor is great. Will there be picket-room in the compound? I have three horses and the bundles and the horse-boy. Moreover, remember that the police here hold me a horse-thief. What do these Lowland

bastards know of horse-thieves? Do you remember that time in Peshawur when Kamel
hammered on the gates of Jumrud—mountebank
that he was—and lifted the colonel's horses all
in one night? Kamel is dead now, but his nephew
has taken up the matter, and there will be more
horses a-missing if the Khaiber Levies do not
look to it.

The peace of God and the favor of his
Prophet be upon this house and all that is in it!
Shanfiz-ullah, rope the mottled mare under the
tree and draw water. The horses can stand in
the sun, but double the felts over the loins. Nay,
my friend, do not trouble to look them over.
They are to sell off to the officer fools who know
so many things of the horse. The mare is heavy
in foal; the gray is a devil unlicked; and the dun—
but you know the trick of the peg. When they
are sold I go back to Pubbi, or, it may be the
Valley of Peshawur.

Oh, friend of my heart, it is good to see
you again. I have been bowing and lying all day
to the officer-sahibs in respect to those horses;
and my mouth is dry for straight talk. *Auggrh!*
Before a meal tobacco is good. Do not join me,
for we are not in our own country. Sit in the
veranda and I will spread my cloth here. But
first I will drink. In the name of God returning
thanks, thrice! This is sweet water, indeed—
sweet as the water of Sheoran when it comes
from the snows.

They are all well and pleased in the North—
Khoda Baksh and the others. Yar Kham has
come down with the horses from Kurdistan—
six-and-thirty head only, and a full half pack-
ponies—and has said openly in the Kashmir Serai
that you English should send guns and blow the
Amir into hell. There are fifteen tolls now on
the Kabul road; and at Dakka, when he thought
he was clear, Yar Khan was stripped of all his
Balkh stallions by the governor! This is a great
injustice, and Yar Khan is hot with rage. And
of the others: Mahbub Ali is still at Pubbi,
writing God knows what. Tuglup Khan is in
jail for the business of the Kohat Police Post.
Faiz Beg came down from Ismailki-Dhera with
a Bokhariot belt for thee, my brother, at the
closing of the year, but none knew whither thou
hadst gone; there was no news left behind. The
cousins have taken a new run near Pakpattan to
breed mules for the government carts, and there
is a story in the Bazar of a priest. Oho! Such a
salt tale! Listen. . . .

Sahib, why do you ask that? My clothes are
fouled because of the dust on the road. My
eyes are sad because of the glare of the sun. My
feet are swollen because I have washed them in
bitter water, and my cheeks are hollow because
the food here is bad. Fire burn your money!
What do I want with it? I am rich and I thought
you were my friend; but you are like the others
—a sahib. Is a man sad? Give him money, say

the sahibs. Is he dishonored? Give him money, say the sahibs. Hath he a wrong upon his head? Give him money, say the sahibs. Such are the sahibs, and such art thou—even thou.

Nay, do not look at the feet of the dun. Pity it is that I ever taught you to know the legs of a horse. Foot-sore? Be it so. What of that? The roads are hard. And the mare foot-sore? She bears a double burden, sahib.

And now I pray you, give me permission to depart. Great favor and honor has the sahib done me, and graciously has he shown his belief that the horses are stolen. Will it please him to send me to the Thana? To call a sweeper and have me led away by one of these lizard-men? I am the sahib's friend. I have drunk water in the shadow of his house, and he has blackened my face. Remains there anything more to do? Will the sahib give me eight annas to make smooth the injury—and complete the insult? . . .

Forgive me, my brother. I knew not—I know not now—what I say. Yes, I lied to you! I will put dust on my head—and I am an Afridi! The horses have been marched foot-sore from the valley to this place, and my eyes are dim, my body aches for the want of sleep, and my heart is dried up with sorrow and shame. But, as it was my shame so by God the Dispenser of Justice—by Allah-al-Mumit, it shall be my own revenge!

We have spoken together with naked hearts

before this, and our hands have dipped into the same dish and thou hast been to me as a brother. Therefore I pay thee back with lies and ingratitude—as a Pathan. Listen now! When the grief of the soul is too heavy for endurance it may be a little eased by speech; and, moreover, the mind of a true man is as a well, and the pebble of confession dropped therein sinks and is no more seen. From the valley have I come on foot, league by league with a fire in my chest like the fire of the Pit. And why? Hast thou, then, so quickly forgotten our customs, among this folk who sell their wives and their daughters for silver? Come back with me to the North and be among men once more. Come back, when this matter is accomplished and I call for thee! The bloom of the peach-orchards is upon all the valley, and here is only dust and a great stink. There is a pleasant wind among the mulberry-trees, and the streams are bright with snow-water, and the caravans go up and the caravans go down, and a hundred fires sparkle in the gut of the pass, and tent-peg answers hammer-nose, and pack-horse squeals to pack-horse across the drift smoke of the evening. It is good in the North now. Come back with me. Let us return to our own people! Come!

*   *   *   *   *   *   *

Whence is my sorrow? Does a man tear out his heart and make fritters thereof over a slow

fire for aught other than a woman? Do not
laugh, friend of mine, for your time will also
be. A woman of the Abazai was she, and I
took her to wife to stanch the feud between our
village and the men of Ghor. I am no longer
young. The lime has touched my beard. True.
I had no need of the wedding? Nay, but I loved
her. What saith Rahman—"Into whose heart
Love enters, there is Folly and naught else. By
a glance of the eye she hath blinded thee; and by
the eyelids and the fringe of the eyelids taken
thee into the captivity without ransom, and naught
else." Dost thou remember that song at the
sheep-roasting in the Pindi camp among the
Uzebegs of the Amir?

The Abazai are dogs and their women the
servants of sin. There was a lover of her own
people, but of that her father told me naught
My friend, curse for me in your prayers, as I
curse at each praying from the Fakr to the Isha,
the name of Daoud Shah, Abazai, whose head is
still upon his neck, whose hands are still upon
his wrists, who has done me dishonor, who has
made my name a laughing-stock among the women
of Little Malikand.

I went into Hindoostan at the end of two
months—to Cherat. I was gone twelve days only;
but I had said that I would be fifteen days absent.
This I did to try her, for it is written: "Trust
not the incapable." Coming up the gorge alone in
the falling of the light, I heard the voice of a man

singing at the door of my house; and it was the
voice of Daoud Shah, and the song that he sung
was "Dray wara yow dee"—all three are one.
It was as though a heel-rope had been slipped
round my heart and all the devils were drawing
it tight past endurance. I crept silently up the
hill-road, but the fuse of my match-lock was
wetted with rain, and I could not slay Daoud Shah
from afar. Moreover, it was in my mind to kill
the woman also. Thus he sung, sitting outside
my house, and, anon, the woman opened the door,
and I came nearer, crawling on my belly among
the rocks. I had only my knife in my hand. But
a stone slipped under my foot, and the two looked
down the hill-side, and he, leaving his match-
lock, fled from my anger, because he was afraid
for the life that was in him. But the woman
moved not till I stood in front of her, crying:
"Oh, woman, what is this that thou hast done?"
And she, void of fear, though she knew my
thought, laughed, saying: "It is a little thing.
I loved him, and thou art a dog and cattle-thief
coming by night. Strike!" And I, being still
blinded by her beauty, for, oh, my friend, the
women of the Abazai are very fair, said: "Hast
thou no fear?" And she answered: "None—
but only the fear that I do not die." Then said
I: "Have no fear." And she bowed her head,
and I smote it off at the neck-bone so that it leaped
between my feet. Thereafter the rage of our
people came upon me, and I hacked off the breasts,

that the men of Little Malikand might know the
crime, and cast the body into the water-course
that flows to the Kabul River. "Dray wara yow
dee! Dray wara yow dee!" The body without
the head, the soul without light, and my own dark-
ling heart—all three are one—all three are one!

That night, making no halt, I went to Ghor
and demanded news of Daoud Shah. Men said:
"He is gone to Pubbi for horses. What wouldst
thou of him? There is peace between the
villages." I made answer: "Ay! The peace of
treachery and the love that the Devil Atla bore
to Gruel." And I fired thrice into the gate and
laughed and went my way.

In those hours, brother and friend of my heart's
heart, the moon and the stars were as blood above
me, and in my mouth was the taste of dry earth.
Also, I broke no bread, and my drink was the
rain of the Valley of Ghor upon my face.

At Pubbi I found Mahbub Ali, the writer,
sitting upon his charpoy and gave up my arms
according to your law. But I was not grieved,
for it was in my heart that I should kill Daoud
Shah with my bare hands thus—as a man strips
a bunch of raisins. Mahbub Ali said: "Daoud
Shah has even now gone hot-foot to Peshawur,
and he will pick up his horses upon the road to
Delhi, for it is said that the Bombay Tramway
Company are buying horses there by the truck-
load; eight horses to the truck." And that was a
true saying.

Then I saw that the hunting would be no little thing, for the man was gone into your borders to save himself against my wrath. And shall he save himself so? Am I not alive? Though he run northward to the Dora and the snow, or southerly to the Black Water, I will follow him, as a lover follows the footsteps of his mistress, and coming upon him I will take him tenderly— Aho! so tenderly!—in my arms, saying: "Well hast thou done and well shalt thou be repaid." And out of that embrace Daoud Shah shall not go forth with the breath in his nostrils. *Auggrh!* Where is the pitcher? I am as thirsty as a mother-mare in the first month.

Your law! What is your law to me? When the horses fight on the runs do they regard the boundry pillars; or do the kites of Ali Musjid forbear because the carrion lies under the shadow of the Ghor Kuttri? The matter began across the border. It shall finish where God pleases. Here, in my own country, or in hell. All three are one.

Listen now, sharer of the sorrow of my heart, and I will tell of the hunting. I followed to Peshawur from Pubbi, and I went to and fro about the streets of Peshawur like a houseless dog, seeking for my enemy. Once I thought that I saw him washing his mouth in the conduit in the big square, but when I came up he was gone. It may be that it was he, and, seeing my face, he had fled.

A girl of the bazaar said that he would go to Nowshera. I said: "Oh, heart's heart, does Daoud Shah visit thee?" and she said: "Even so." I said: "I would fain see him, for we be friends parted for two years. Hide me, I pray, here in the shadow of the window shutter, and I will wait for his coming." And the girl said: "Oh, Pathan, look into my eyes!" And I turned, leaning upon her breast, and looked into her eyes, swearing that I spoke the very Truth of God. But she answered: "Never friend waited friend with such eyes. Lie to God and the Prophet, but to a woman ye can not lie. Get hence! There shall no harm befall Daoud Shah by cause of me."

I would have strangled that girl but for the fear of your police; and thus the hunting would have come to naught. Therefore I only laughed and departed, and she leaned over the window-bar in the night and mocked me down the street. Her name is Jamun. When I have made my account with the man I will return to Peshawur and—her lovers shall desire her no more for her beauty's sake. She shall not be Jamun, but Ak, the cripple among trees. Ho! Ho! Ak shall she be!

At Peshawur I bought the horses and grapes, and the almonds and dried fruits, that the reason of my wonderings might be open to the government, and that there might be no hinderance upon the road. But when I came to Nowshera he was gone, and I knew not where to go. I stayed one day at Nowshera, and in the night a voice spoke in my ear as I slept among the horses. All night it flew round my head and would not cease from whispering. I was upon my belly, sleeping as the devils sleep, and it may have been that the voice was the voice of a devil. It said: "Go south, and thou shalt come upon Daoud Shah." Listen, my brother and chiefest among friends— listen! Is the tale a long one? Think how it was long to me. I have trodden every league of the road from Pubbi to this place; and from Nowshera my guide was only the voice and the lust of vengeance.

To the Uttock I went, but that was no hinderance to me. Ho! Ho! A man may turn the word twice, even in his trouble. The Uttock was no *uttock* (obstacle) to me; and I heard the voice above the noise of the waters beating on the big rock, saying: "Go to the right." So I went to Pindigheb, and those days my sleep was taken from me utterly, and the head of the woman of the Abazai was before me night and day, even as it had fallen between my feet. "Dray wara yow dee! Dray wara yow dee!" Fire, ashes, and my couch, all three are one—all three are one!

Now I was far from the winter path of the dealers who had gone to Sialkot and so south by the rail and the Big Road to the line of cantonments; but there was a sahib in camp at Pindigheb who bought from me a white mare at a good price, and told me that one Daoud Shah had passed to Shahpur with horses. Then I saw that the warning of the voice was true, and made swift to come to the Salt Hills. The Jhelum was in flood, but I could not wait, and, in the crossing, a bay stallion was washed down and drowned. Herein was God hard to me—not in respect of the beast, of that I had no care—but in this snatching. While I was upon the right bank urging the horses into the water, Daoud Shah was upon the left; for—*Alghias! Alghias!*—the hoofs of my mare scattered the hot ashes of his fires when we came up the hither bank in the light of morning. But he had fled. His feet were made swift by the terror of death. And I went south from Shahpur as the kite flies. I dared not turn aside, lest I should miss my vengeance—which is my right. From Shahpur I skirted by the Jhelum, for I thought that he would avoid the Desert of the Rechna. But, presently, at Sahiwal, I turned away upon the road to Jhang, Samundri, and Gugera, till, upon a night, the mottled mare breasted the fence of the rail that runs to Montgomery. And that place was Okara, and the head of the woman of the Abazai lay upon the sand between my feet.

Thence I went to Fazilka, and they said that I was mad to bring starved horses there. The Voice was with me, and I was not mad, but only wearied, because I could not find Daoud Shah. It was written that I should not find him at Rania

nor Bahadurgah, and I came into Delhi from
the west, and there also I found him not. My
friend, I have seen many strange things in my
wanderings. I have seen devils rioting across
the Rechna as the stallions riot in spring. I have
heard the Djinns calling to each other from the
holes in the sand, and I have seen them pass before
my face. There are no devils, say the sahibs?
They are very wise, but they do not know all
things about devils or—horses. Ho! Ho! I say
to you who are laughing at my misery, that I
have seen the devils at high noon whooping and
leaping on the shoals of the Chenab. And was I
afraid? My brother, when the desire of a man
is set upon one thing alone, he fears neither God
nor man nor devil. If my vengeance failed, I
would splinter the gates of paradise with the butt
of my gun, or I would cut my way into hell with
my knife, and I would call upon those who govern
there for the body of Daoud Shah. What love
so deep as hate?

Do not speak. I know the thought in your
heart. Is the white of this eye clouded? How
does the blood beat at the wrist? There is no
madness in my flesh, but only the vehemence of
the desire that has eaten me up. Listen!

South of Delhi I knew not the country at all.
Therefore I can not say where I went, but I
passed through many cities. I knew only that
it was laid upon me to go south. When the horses
could march no more, I threw myself upon the

earth, and waited till the day. There was no sleep with me in that journeying; and that was a heavy burden. Dost thou know, brother of mine, the evil of wakefulness that can not break —when the bones are sore for lack of sleep, and the skin of the temples twitches with weariness, and yet—there is no sleep—there is no sleep? "Dray wara yow dee! Dray wara yow dee!" The eye of the sun, the eye of the moon, and my own unrestful eyes—all three are one—all three are one!

There was a city the name whereof I have forgotten, and there the Voice called all night. That was ten days ago. It has cheated me afresh.

I have come hither from a place called Hamirpur, and, behold, it was my fate that I should meet with thee to my comfort, and the increase of friendship. This is a good omen. By the joy of looking upon thy face the weariness has gone from my feet, and the sorrow of my so long travel is forgotten. Also my heart is peaceful; for I know that the end is near.

It may be that I shall find Daoud Shah in this city going northward, since a Hillman will ever head back to his hills when the spring warns. And shall he see those hills of our country? Surely I shall overtake him! Surely my vengeance is safe! Surely God hath him in the hollow of His hand against my claiming. There shall no harm befall Daoud Shah till I come; for I would fain kill him quick and whole with the life sticking firm in his body. A pomegranate is sweetest when the cloves break away unwilling from the rind. Let it be in the day-time, that I may see his face, and my delight may be crowned.

And when I have accomplished the matter and my honor is made clean, I shall return thanks unto God, the holder of the scale of the law, and I shall sleep. From the night, through the day, and into the night again I shall sleep; and no dream shall trouble me.

And now, oh, my brother, the tale is all told. *Ahi! Ahi! Alghias! Ahi!*

AT TWENTY-TWO

NARROW as the womb, deep as the Pit, and dark as the heart of a man.—*Sonthal Miner's Proverb.*

"A WEAVER went out to reap but stayed to unravel the corn-stalks. Ha! ha! ha! Is there any sense in a weaver?"

The never-ending tussle had recommenced. Janki Meah glared at Kundoo, but, as Janki Meah was blind, Kundoo was not impressed. He had come to argue with Janki Meah, and, if chance favored, to make love to the old man's beautiful young wife.

This was Kundoo's grievance, and he spoke in the name of all the five men who, with Janki Meah, composed the gang in No. 7 gallery of Twenty-two. Janki Meah had been blind for thirty years during which he had served the Jimahari Collieries with pick and crowbar. All through those thirty years he had regularly, every morning before going down, drawn from the overseer his allowance of lamp-oil—just as if he had been an eyed miner. What Kundoo's gang resented, as hundreds of gangs had resented before, was Janki Meah's selfishness. He would not add the oil to the common stock of his gang, but would save and sell it.

"I knew these workings before you were born,"
Janki Meah used to reply: "I don't want the light
to get my coal out by, and I am not going to help
you. The oil is mine, and I intend to keep it."

A strange man in many ways was Janki
Meah, the white-haired, hot-tempered, sightless
weaver who had turned pitman. All day long—
except on Sundays and Mondays, when he was
usually drunk—he worked in the Twenty-two
shaft of the Jimahari Colliery as cleverly as a
man with all the senses. At evening he went up
in the great steam-hauled cage to the pit-bank,
and there called for his pony—a rusty, coal-dusty
beast, nearly as old as Janki Meah. The pony
would come to his side, and Janki Meah would
clamber on to its back and be taken at once to
the plot of land which he, like the other miners,
received from the Jimahari company. The pony
knew that place, and when, after six years, the
company changed all the allotments to prevent
the miners acquiring proprietary rights, Janki
Meah represented, with tears in his eyes, that
were his holding shifted he would never be able
to find his way to a new one. "My horse only
knows that place," pleaded Janki Meah, and so
he was allowed to keep his land.

On the strength of this concession and his
accumulated oil-savings, Janki Meah took a
second wife—a girl of the Jolaha main stock of
the Meahs, and singularly beautiful. Janki Meah
could not see her beauty; wherefore he took her

on trust, and forbade her to go down the pit. He
had not worked for thirty years in the dark without knowing that the pit was no place for pretty
women. He loaded her with ornaments—not
brass or pewter, but real silver ones—and she
rewarded him by flirting outrageously with
Kundoo of No. 7 gallery-gang. Kundoo was
really the gang head, but Janki Meah insisted
upon all the work being entered in his own name,
and chose the men that he worked with. Custom
—stronger even than the Jimahari company—
dictated that Janki, by right of his years, should
manage these things, and should also work despite
his blindness. In Indian mines where they cut
into the solid coal with the pick and clear it out
from floor to ceiling, he could come to no great
harm. At home, where they undercut the coal,
and bring it down in crashing avalanches from
the roof, he would never have been allowed to
set foot in a pit. He was not a popular man, because of his oil-savings; but all the gangs admitted
that Janki knew all the *khads*, or workings, that
had ever been sunk or worked since the Jimahari
company first started operations on the Tarachunda fields.

Pretty little Unda only knew that her old
husband was a fool who could be managed. She
took no interest in the collieries except in so far
as they swallowed up Kundoo five days out of
the seven, and covered him with coal-dust. Kundoo was a great workman, and did his best not

to get drunk, because, when he had saved forty rupees, Unda was to steal everything that she could find in Janki's house and run with Kundoo "over the hills and far away" to countries where there were no mines, and every one kept three fat bullocks and a milch-buffalo. While this scheme was maturing it was his amiable custom to drop in upon Janki and worry him about the oil-savings. Unda sat in a corner and nodded approval. On the night when Kundoo had quoted that objectionable proverb about weavers, Janki grew angry.

"Listen, you pig," said he, "blind I am, and old I am, but, before ever you were born, I was gray among the coal. Even in the days when the Twenty-two *khad* was unsunk and there were not two thousand men here, I was known to have all knowledge of the pits. What *khad* is there that I do not know, from the bottom of the shaft to the end of the last drive? Is it the Baromba *khad*, the oldest, or the Twenty-two where Tibu's gallery runs up to Number 5?"

"Hear the old fool talk," said Kundoo, nodding to Unda. "No gallery of Twenty-two will cut into five before the end of the rains. We have a month's solid coal before us. The Babuji says so."

"Babuji! Pigji! Dogji! What do these fat slugs from Calcutta know? He draws and draws and draws, and talks and talks and talks, and his maps are all wrong. I, Janki, know that this is

so. When a man has been shut up in the dark
for thirty years, God gives him knowledge. The
old gallery that Tibu's gang made is not six feet
from Number 5."

"Without doubt God gives the blind knowledge," said Kundoo, with a look at Unda. "Let
it be as you say. I, for my part, do not know
where lies the gallery of Tibu's gang, but I am
not a withered monkey who needs oil to grease
his joints with."

Kundoo swung out of the hut laughing, and
Unda giggled. Janki turned his sightless eyes
toward his wife and swore. "I have land, and
I have sold a great deal of lamp-oil," mused Janki;
"but I was a fool to marry this child."

A week later the rains set in with a vengeance,
and the gangs paddled about in coal-slush at the
pit-banks. Then the big mine-pumps were made
ready, and the manager of the colliery plowed
through the wet toward the Tarachunda River
swelling between its soppy banks. "Lord, send
that this beastly beck doesn't misbehave," said
the manager, piously, and he went and took
counsel with his assistant about the pumps.

But the Tarachunda misbehaved very much
indeed. After a fall of three inches of rain in
an hour it was obliged to do something. It topped
its bank and joined the flood-water that was
hemmed between two low hills just where the
embankment of the colliery main line crossed.
When a good part of a rain-fed river, and a few

acres of flood-water, make a dead set for a nine-foot culvert, the culvert may spout its finest, but the water can not all get out. The manager pranced upon one leg with excitement, and his language was improper.

He had reason to swear, because he knew that one inch of water on land meant a pressure of one hundred tons to the acre; and here were about five feet of water forming, behind the railway embankment, over the shallower workings of Twenty-two. You must understand that, in a coal-mine, the coal nearest the surface is worked first from the central shaft. That is to say, the miners may clear out the stuff to within ten, twenty, or thirty feet, of the surface, and, when all is worked out, leave only a skin of earth upheld by some few pillars of coal. In a deep mine where they know that they have any amount of material at hand, men prefer to get all their mineral out at one shaft, rather than make a number of little holes to tap the comparatively unimportant surface coal.

And the manager watched the flood.

The culvert spouted a nine-foot gush; but the water still formed, and word was sent to clear the men out of Twenty-two. The cages came up crammed and crammed again with the men nearest the pit-eye, as they call the place where you can see daylight from the bottom of the main shaft. All away and away, up the long black galleries the flare-lamps were winking and dancing like so many fire-flies, and the men and the women waited for the clanking, rattling, thundering cages to come down and fly up again. But the out-workings were very far off, and the word could not be passed quickly, though the heads of the gangs and the assistant shouted and swore and tramped and stumbled. The manager kept one eye on the great troubled pool behind the embankment, and prayed that the culvert would give way and let the water through in time. With the other eye he watched the cages come up and saw the headmen counting the roll of the gangs. With all his heart and soul he swore at the winder who controlled the iron drum that wound up the wire rope on which hung the cages.

In a little time there was a down-draw in the water behind the embankment—a sucking whirlpool, all yellow and yeasty. The water had smashed through the skin of the earth and was pouring into the old shallow workings of Twenty-two.

Deep down below, a rush of black water caught the last gang waiting for the cage, and as they clambered in, the whirl was about their waists. The cage reached the pit-bank, and the manager called the roll. The gangs were all safe except Gang Janki, Gang Mogul, and Gang Rahim, eighteen men, with perhaps ten basket-women who loaded the coal into the little iron carriages that ran on the tramways of the main galleries. These gangs were in the out-workings, three quarters of a mile away, on the extreme fringe of the mine. Once more the cage went down, but with only two Englishmen in it, and dropped into a swirling, roaring current that had almost touched the roof of some of the lower side-galleries. One of the wooden balks with which they had propped the old workings shot past on the current, just missing the cage.

"If we don't want our ribs knocked out, we'd better go," said the manager. "We can't even save the company's props."

The cage drew out of the water with a splash, and a few minutes later, it was officially reported that there were at least ten feet of water in the pit's-eye. Now ten feet of water there meant that all other places in the mine were flooded except such galleries as were more than ten feet above the level of the bottom of the shaft. The deep workings would be full, the main galleries would be full, but in the high workings reached by inclines from the main roads, there would be a certain amount of air cut off, so to speak, by the water and squeezed up by it. The little science-primers explain how water behaves when you pour it down test-tubes. The flooding of Twenty-two was an illustration on a large scale.

* * * * * * *

"By the Holy Grove, what has happened to the air? It was a Sonthal gangman of Gang Mogul in No. 9 gallery, and he was driving a six-foot way through the coal. Then there was a rush from the other galleries, and Gang Janki and Gang Rahim stumbled up with their basket-women.

"Water has come in the mine," they said, "and there is no way of getting out."

"I went down," said Janki—"down the slope of my gallery, and I felt the water."

"There has been no water in the cutting in our time," clamored the women. "Why can not we go away?"

"Be silent," said Janki; "long ago, when my father was here, water came to Ten—no, Eleven—cutting, and there was great trouble. Let us get away to where the air is better."

The three gangs and the basket-women left No. 9 gallery and went further up No. 16. At one turn of the road they could see the pitchy black water lapping on the coal. It had touched the roof of a gallery that they knew well—a gallery where they used to smoke their *huqas* and conduct their flirtations. Seeing this, they called aloud upon their gods, and the Meahs, who are thrice bastard Mohammedans, strove to recollect the name of the Prophet. They came to a great open square whence nearly all the coal had been extracted. It was the end of the out-workings, and the end of the mine.

Far away down the gallery a small pumping-engine, used for keeping dry a deep working and fed with steam from above, was faithfully throbbing. They heard it cease.

"They have cut off the steam," said Kundoo, hopefully. "They have given the order to use all the steam for the pit-bank pumps. They will clear out the water."

"If the water has reached the smoking-gallery," said Janki, "all the company's pumps can do nothing for three days."

"It is very hot," moaned Jasoda, the Meah basket-woman. "There is a very bad air here because of the lamps."

"Put them out," said Janki; "why do you want lamps?" The lamps were put out amid protests, and the company sat still in the utter dark. Somebody rose quietly and began walking over the coals. It was Janki, who was touching the walls with his hands. "Where is the ledge?" he murmured to himself.

"Sit, sit!" said Kundoo. "If we die, we die. The air is very bad."

But Janki still stumbled and crept and tapped with his pick upon the walls. The women rose to their feet.

"Stay all where you are. Without the lamps you can not see, and I—I am always seeing." said Janki. Then he paused, and called out: "Oh, you who have been in the cutting more than ten years, what is the name of this open place? I am an old man and I have forgotten."

"Bullia's Room," answered the Sonthal who had complained of the vileness of the air.

"Again," said Janki.

"Bullia's Room."

"Then I have found it," said Janki. "The name only had slipped my memory. Tibu's gang's gallery is here."

"A lie," said Kundoo. "There have been no galleries in this place since my day."

"Three paces was the depth of the ledge," muttered Janki without heeding—"and—oh, my poor bones!—I have found it! It is here, up this ledge. Come all you, one by one, to the place of my voice, and I will count you."

There was a rush in the dark, and Janki felt the first man's face hit his knees as the Sonthal scrambled up the ledge.

"Who?" cried Janki.

"I, Sunua Manji."

"Sit you down," said Janki. "Who next?"

One by one the women and the men crawled up the ledge which ran along one side of "Bullia's Room." Degraded Mohammedan, pig-eating Musahr and wild Sonthal, Janki ran his hand over them all.

"Now follow after," said he, "catching hold of my heel, and the women catching the men's clothes." He did not ask whether the men had brought their picks with them. A miner, black or white, does not drop his pick. One by one, Janki leading, they crept into the old gallery—a six-foot way with a scant four feet from thill to roof.

"The air is better here," said Jasoda. They could hear her heart beating in thick, sick bumps.

"Slowly, slowly," said Janki. "I am an old man, and I forget many things. This is Tibu's gallery, but where are the four bricks where they used to put their huqa fire on when the sahibs never saw? Slowly, slowly, oh, you people behind."

They heard his hands disturbing the small coal on the floor of the gallery and then a dull sound. "This is one unbaked brick, and this is another and another. Kundoo is a young man—let him come forward. Put a knee upon this brick and strike here. When Tibu's gang were at dinner on the last day before the good coal ended, they heard the men of Five on the other side, and Five worked their gallery two Sundays later—or it may have been one. Strike there, Kundoo, but give me room to go back."

Kundoo, doubting, drove the pick, but the first soft crush of the coal was a call to him. He was fighting for his life and for Unda—pretty little Unda with the rings on all her toes—for Unda and the forty rupees. The woman sang the "Song of the Pick"—the terrible, slow, swinging melody with the muttered chorus that repeats the sliding of the loosened coal, and, to each cadence, Kundoo smote in the black dark. When he could do no

more, Sunua Manji took the pick, and struck for
his life and his wife, and his village beyond the
blue hills over the Tarachunda River. An hour
the men worked, and then the women cleared
away the coal.

"It is further than I thought," said Janki.
"The air is very bad; but strike, Kundoo, strike
hard."

For the fifth time Kundoo took up the pick
as the Sonthal crawled back. The song had
scarcely recommenced when it was broken by a
yell from Kundoo that echoed down the gallery:
"Par hua! Par hua! We are through, we are
through!" The imprisoned air in the mine shot
through the opening, and the women at the far
end of the gallery heard the water rush through
the pillars of "Bullia's Room" and roar against
the ledge. Having fulfilled the law under which
it worked, it rose no further. The women
screamed and pressed forward. "The water has
come—we shall be killed! Let us go."

Kundoo crawled through the gap and found
himself in a propped gallery by the simple process
of hitting his head against a beam.

"Do I know the pits or do I not?" chuckled
Janki. "This is the Number Five; go you out
slowly, giving me your names. Ho! Rahim,
count your gang! Now let us go forward, each
catching hold of the other as before."

They formed a line in the darkness and Janki
led them—for a pitman in a strange pit is only

one degree less liable to err than an ordinary mortal underground for the first time. At last they saw a flare-lamp, and Gangs Janki, Mogul and Rahim of Twenty-two stumbled dazed into the glare of the draught-furnace at the bottom of Five: Janki feeling his way and the rest behind.

"Water has come into Twenty-two. God knows where are the others. I have brought these men from Tibu's gallery in our cutting; making connection through the north side of the gallery. Take us to the cage," said Janki Meah.

*   *   *   *   *   *   *

At the pit-bank of Twenty-two, some thousand people clamored and wept and shouted. One hundred men—one thousand men—had been drowned in the cutting. They would all go to their homes to-morrow. Where were their men? Little Unda, her scarf drenched with the rain, stood at the pit-mouth calling down the shaft for Kundoo. They had swung the cages clear of the mouth, and her only answer was the murmur of the flood in the pit's-eye two hundred and sixty feet below.

"Look after that woman! She'll chuck herself down the shaft in a minute," shouted the manager.

But he need not have troubled; Unda was afraid of death. She wanted Kundoo. The assistant was watching the flood and seeing how far he could wade into it. There was a lull in the water, and the whirlpool had slackened. The mine was full, and the people at the pit-bank howled.

"My faith, we shall be lucky if we have five hundred hands in the place to-morrow!" said the manager. "There's some chance yet of running a temporary dam across that water. Shove in anything—tubs and bullock-carts if you haven't enough bricks. Make them work now if they never worked before. Hi! you gangers, make them work."

Little by little the crowd was broken into detachments, and pushed toward the water with promises of overtime. The dam-making began, and when it was fairly under way, the manager thought that the hour had come for the pumps. There was no fresh inrush into the mine. The tall, red, iron-clamped pump-beam rose and fell, and the pumps snored and guttered and shrieked as the first water poured out of the pipe.

"We must run her all to-night," said the manager, wearily, "but there's no hope for the poor devils down below. Look here, Gur Sahai, if you are proud of your engines, show me what they can do now."

Gur Sahai grinned and nodded, with his right hand upon the lever and an oil-can in his left. He could do no more than he was doing, but he could keep that up till the dawn. Were the company's pumps to be beaten by the vagaries of that troublesome Tarachunda River? Never, never! And the pumps sobbed and panted: "Never, never!" The manager sat in the shelter of the pit-bank roofing, trying to dry himself by the pump-boiler fire, and, in the dreary dusk, he saw the crowds on the dam scatter and fly.

"That's the end," he groaned. " 'Twill take us six weeks to persuade 'em that we haven't tried to drown their mates on purpose. Oh, for a decent, rational Geordie!"

But the flight had no panic in it. Men had run over from Five with astounding news, and the foremen could not hold their gangs together. Presently, surrounded by a clamorous crew, Gangs Rahim, Mogul, and Janki, and ten basket-women, walked up to report themselves, and pretty little Unda stole away to Janki's hut to prepare his evening meal.

"Alone I found the way," explained Janki Meah, "and now will the Company give me pension?"

The simple pit-folk shouted and leaped and went back to the dam, reassured in their old belief that, whatever happened, so great was the power of the Company whose salt they ate, none of them could be killed. But Gur Sahai only bared his white teeth and kept his hand upon the lever and proved his pumps to the uttermost.

*　*　*　*　*　*　*

"I say," said the Assistant to the Manager, a week later, "do you recollect Germinal?"

"Yes. 'Queer thing. I thought of it in the cage when that balk went by. Why?"

"Oh, this business seems to be Germinal upside down. Janki was in my veranda all this morning, telling me that Kundoo had eloped with his wife—Unda, or Anda, I think her name was."

"Hillo! And those were the cattle that you risked your life to clear out of Twenty-Two!"

"No—I was thinking of the Company's props, not the Company's men."

"Sounds better to say so now; but I don't believe you, old fellow."

ON THE CITY WALL

THEN she let them down by a cord through the window; for her house was upon the town wall, and she dwelt upon the wall.—*Joshua* ii. 15.

LALUN is a member of the most ancient profession in the world. Lilith was her very-great-grandmamma, and that was before the days of Eve as every one knows. In the West, people say rude things about Lalun's profession, and write lectures about it, and distribute the lectures to young persons in order that morality may be preserved. In the East, where the profession is hereditary, descending from mother to daughter, nobody writes lectures or takes any notice, and that is a distinct proof of the inability of the East to manage its own affairs.

Lalun's real husband, for even ladies of Lalun's profession in the East must have husbands, was a great, big jujube-tree. Her mamma, who had married a fig, spent ten thousand rupees on Lalun's wedding, which was blessed by forty-seven clergymen of mamma's church, and distributed five thousand rupees in charity to the poor. And that was the custom of the land. The advantages of having a jujube-tree for a husband are obvious. You can not hurt his feelings, and he looks imposing.

Lalun's husband stood on the plain outside the city walls, and Lalun's house was upon the east wall facing the river. If you fell from the broad window-seat you dropped thirty feet sheer into the city ditch. But if you stayed where you should and looked forth, you saw all the cattle of the city being driven down to water, the students of the government college playing cricket, the high grass and trees that fringed the river-bank, the great sand-bars that ribbed the river, the red tombs of dead emperors beyond the river, and very far away through the blue heat-haze, a glint of the snows of the Himalayas.

Wali Dad used to lie in the window-seat for hours at a time watching this view. He was a young Mohammedan who was suffering acutely from education of the English variety and knew it. His father had sent him to a mission-school to get wisdom, and Wali Dad had absorbed more than ever his father or the missionaries intended he should. When his father died, Wali Dad was independent and spent two years experimenting with the creeds of the earth and reading books that are of no use to anybody.

After he had made an unsuccessful attempt to enter the Roman Catholic Church and the Presbyterian fold at the same time (the missionaries found him out and called him names, but they didn't understand his trouble), he discovered Lalun on the city wall and became the most constant of her few admirers. He possessed a head that English artists at home would rave over and paint amid impossible surroundings—a face that female novelists would use with delight through nine hundred pages. In reality he was only a clean-bred young Mohammedan, with penciled eyebrows, small-cut nostrils, little feet and hands, and a very tired look in his eyes. By virtue of his twenty-two years he had grown a neat black beard which he stroked with pride and kept delicately scented. His life seemed to be divided between borrowing books from me and making love to Lalun in the window-seat. He composed songs about her, and some of the songs are sung to this day in the city from the street of the mutton-butchers to the copper-smith's ward.

One song, the prettiest of all, says that the beauty of Lalun was so great that it troubled the hearts of the British government and caused them to lose their peace of mind. That is the way the song is sung in the streets; but, if you examine it carefully and know the key to the explanation, you will find that there are three puns in it—on "beauty," "heart," and "peace of mind"— so that it runs: "By the subtlety of Lalun the administration of the government was troubled and it lost such and such a man." When Wali Dad sings that song his eyes glow like hot coals and Lalun leans back among the cushions and throws bunches of jasmine buds at Wali Dad.

But first it is necessary to explain something about the supreme government which is above all and below all and behind all. Gentlemen come from England, spend a few weeks in India, walk round this great Sphinx of the Plains, and write books upon its ways and its works, denouncing or praising it as their own ignorance prompts. Consequently all the world knows how the supreme government conducts itself. But no one, not even the supreme government, knows everything about the administration of the empire. Year by year England sends out fresh drafts for the first fighting-line, which is officially called the Indian Civil Service. These die, or kill themselves by overwork, or are worried to death or broken in health and hope in order that the land may be protected from death and sickness, famine and war, and may eventually become capable of standing alone. It will never stand alone, but the idea is a pretty one, and men are willing to die for it, and yearly the work of pushing and coaxing and scolding and petting the country into good living goes forward. If an advance be made all credit is given to the native, while the Englishmen stand back and wipe their foreheads. If a failure occurs the Englishmen step forward and take the blame. Overmuch tenderness of this kind has bred a strong belief among many natives that the native is capable of administering the country, and many devout Englishmen believe this also, because the theory is stated in beautiful English with all the latest political garnish.

There be other men who, though uneducated,

see visions and dream dreams, and they, too, hope
to administer the country in their own way—that
is to say, with a garnish of red sauce. Such men
must exist among two hundred million people,
and, if they are not attended to, may cause trouble
and even break the great idol called "Pax Britan-
nic," which, as the newspapers say, lives between
Peshawur and Cape Comorin. Were the day of
doom to dawn to-morrow, you would find the
supreme government "taking measures to allay
popular excitement" and putting guards upon the
grave-yards that the dead might troop forth
orderly. The youngest civilian would arrest
Gabriel on his own responsibility if the archangel
could not produce a deputy commissioner's permission to "make music or other noises," as the
form says.

Whence it is easy to see that mere men of the
flesh who would create a tumult must fare badly
at the hands of the supreme government. And
they do. There is no outward sign of excitement;
there is no confusion; there is no knowledge.
When due and sufficient reasons have been given,
weighed and approved, the machinery moves forward, and the dreamer of dreams and the seer
of visions is gone from his friends and following. He enjoys the hospitality of government;
there is no restriction upon his movements within
certain limits; but he must not confer any more
with his brother dreamers. Once in every six
months the supreme government assures itself

that he is well and takes formal acknowledgment of his existence. No one protests against his detention, because the few people who know about it are in deadly fear of seeming to know him; and never a single newspaper "takes up his case," or organizes demonstrations on his behalf, because the newspapers of India have got behind that lying proverb which says the pen is mightier than the sword, and can walk delicately and with circumspection.

So now you know as much as you ought about Wali Dad, the educational mixture, and the supreme government.

Lalun has not yet been described. She would need, so Wali Dad says, a thousand pens of gold and ink scented with musk. She has been variously compared to the moon, the Dil Sagar Lake, a spotted quail, a gazelle, the sun on the Desert of Kutch, the dawn, the stars, and the young bamboo. These comparisons imply that she is beautiful exceedingly according to the native standards, which are practically the same as those of the West. Her eyes are black and her hair is black, and her eyebrows are black as leeches; her mouth is tiny and says witty things; her hands are tiny and have saved much money; her feet are tiny and have trodden on the naked hearts of many men. But, as Wali Dad sings: "Lalun is Lalun, and when you have said that, you have only come to the beginnings of knowledge."

The little house on the city wall was just big

enough to hold Lalun, and her maid, and a pussy-cat with a silver collar. A big pink and blue cut-glass chandelier hung from the ceiling of the reception-room. A petty Nawab had given Lalun the horror, and she kept it for politeness' sake. The floor of the room was of polished chunam, white as curds. A latticed window of carved wood was set in one wall; there was a profusion of squabby pluffy cushions and fat carpets everywhere, and Lalun's silver huqa, studded with turquoises, had a special little carpet all to its shining self. Wali Dad was nearly as permanent a fixture as the chandelier. As I have said, he lay in the window-seat and meditated on life and death and Lalun—'specially Lalun. The feet of the young men of the city tended to her door-ways and then—retired, for Lalun was a particular maiden, slow of speech, reserved of mind, and not in the least inclined to orgies which were nearly certain to end in strife. "If I am of no value, I am unworthy of this honor," said Lalun. "If I am of value, they are unworthy of me." And that was a crooked sentence.

In the long hot nights of latter April and May all the city seemed to assemble in Lalun's little white room to smoke and to talk. Shiahs of the grimmest and most uncompromising persuasion; Sufis who had lost all belief in the Prophet and retained but little in God; wandering Hindoo priests passing southward on their way to the Central India fairs and other affairs; pundits in black gowns, with spectacles on their noses and undigested wisdom in their insides; bearded headmen of the wards; Sikhs with all the details of the latest ecclesiastical scandal in the Golden Temple; red-eyed priests from beyond the border, looking like trapped wolves and talking like ravens; M. A.'s of the university, very superior and very voluble—all these people and more also you might find in the white room. Wali Dad lay in the window-seat and listened to the talk.

"It is Lalun's salon," said Wali Dad to me, "and it is eclectic—is not that the word? Outside of a Freemason's lodge I have never seen such gatherings. There I dined once with a Jew—a Yahoudi!" He spat into the city ditch with apologies for allowing national feelings to overcome him. "Tho' I have lost every belief in the world," said he, "and try to be proud of my losing, I can not help hating a Jew. Lalun admits no Jews here."

"But what in the world do all these men do?"

"The curse of our country," said Wali Dad. "They talk. It is like the Athenians—always hearing and telling some new thing. Ask the Pearl and she will show you how much she knows of the news of the city and the province. Lalun knows everything."

"Lalun," I said at random—she was talking to a gentleman of the Kurd persuasion who had come in from God knows where—"when does the 175th Regiment go to Agra?"

"It does not go at all," said Lalun, without

turning her head. "They have ordered the 118th
to go instead. That Regiment goes to Lucknow
in three months unless they give a fresh order."

"That is so," said Wali Dad, without a shade
of doubt. "Can you, with your telegrams and
your newspapers, do better? Always hearing and
telling some new thing," he went on. "My friend,
has your God ever smitten a European nation for
gossiping in the bazaars? India has gossiped for
centuries—always standing in the bazaars until
the soldiers go by. Therefore . . . you are
here to-day instead of starving in your own country, and I am not a Mohammedan—I am a product—a 'demnition' product. That also I owe
to you and yours; that I can not make an end
to any sentence without quoting from your
authors." He pulled at the huqa and mourned,
half feelingly, half in earnest, for the shattered
hopes of his youth. Wali Dad was always mourning over something or other—the country of
which he despaired, or the creed in which he had
lost faith, or the life of the English which he
could by no means understand.

Lalun never mourned. She played little songs
on the *sitar,* and to hear her sing, "Oh, Peacock,
Cry Again," was always a fresh pleasure. She
knew all the songs that have ever been sung, from
the war-songs of the south that make the old men
angry with the young men and the young men
angry with the state, to the love songs of the
north where the swords whinny-whicker like

angry kites in the pauses between the kisses, and
the passes fill with armed men, and the lover is
torn from his beloved and cries *Ai! Ai! Ai!* ever-
more. She knew how to make up tobacco for the
huqa so that it smelled like the gates of paradise
and wafted you gently through them. She could
embroider strange things in gold and silver, and
dance softly with the moonlight when it came in
at the window. Also she knew the hearts of men,
and the heart of the city, and whose wives were
faithful and whose untrue, and more of the secrets
of the government offices than are good to be set
down in this place. Nasiban, her maid, said that
her jewelry was worth ten thousand pounds, and
that, some night, a thief would enter and murder
her for its possession; but Lalun said that all the
city would tear that thief limb from limb, and
that he, whoever he was, knew it.

So she took her *sitar* and sat in the window-
seat and sung a song of old days that had been
sung by a girl of her profession in an armed camp
on the eve of a great battle—the day before the
fords of the Jumna ran red and Sivaji fled fifty
miles to Delhi with a Toorkh stallion at his horse's
tail and another Lalun on his saddle-bow. It was
what men call a Mahratta *laonee*, and it said:

> Their warrior forces Chimnajee
>   Before the Peishwa led,
> The Children of the Sun and Fire
>   Behind him turned and fled.

And the chorus said:

> With them there fought who rides so free
> With sword and turban red,
> The warrior-youth who earns his fee
> At peril of his head.

"At peril of his head," said Wali Dad in English to me. "Thanks to your government, all our heads are protected, and with the educational facilities at my command"—his eyes twinkled wickedly—"I might be a distinguished member of the local administration. Perhaps, in time, I might even be a member of a legislative council."

"Don't speak English," said Lalun, bending over her *sitar* afresh. The chorus went out from the city wall to the blackened wall of Fort Amara which dominates the city. No man knows the precise extent of Fort Amara. Three kings built it hundreds of years ago, and they say that there are miles of underground rooms beneath its walls. It is peopled with many ghosts, a detachment of garrison artillery and a company of infantry. In its prime it held ten thousand men and filled its ditches with corpses.

"At peril of his head," sung Lalun again and again.

A head moved on one of the ramparts—the gray head of an old man—and a voice, rough as shark-skin on a sword-hilt, sent back the last line of the chorus and broke into a song that I could not understand, though Lalun and Wali Dad listened intently.

"What is it?" I asked. "Who is it?"

"A consistent man," said Wali Dad. "He fought you in '46, when he was a warrior-youth; refought you in '57, and he tried to fight you in '71, but you had learned the trick of blowing men from guns too well. Now he is old; but he would still fight if he could."

"Is he a Wahabi, then? Why should he answer to a Mahratta *laonee* if he be Wahabi—or Sikh?" said I.

"I do not know," said Wali Dad. "He has lost, perhaps, his religion. Perhaps he wishes to be a king. Perhaps he is a king. I do not know his name."

"That is a lie, Wali Dad. If you know his career you must know his name."

"That is quite true. I belong to a nation of liars. I would rather not tell you his name. Think for yourself."

Lalun finished her song, pointed to the fort and said simply: "Khem Singh."

"H'm," said Wali Dad. "If the Pearl chooses to tell you the Pearl is a fool."

I translated to Lalun, who laughed. "I choose to tell what I choose to tell. They kept Khem Singh in Burmah," said she. "They kept him there for many years until his mind was changed in him. So great was the kindness of the government. Finding this, they sent him back to his own country that he might look upon it before he died. He is an old man, but when he looks upon this his country his memory will come. Moreover, there be many who remember him."

"He is an interesting survival," said Wali Dad, pulling at the *huqa*. "He returns to a country now full of educational and political reform, but, as the Pearl says, there are many who remember him. He was once a great man. There will never be any more great men in India. They will all, when they are boys, go whoring after strange gods, and they will become citizens—'fellow-citizens'—'illustrious fellow-citizens.' What is it that the native papers call them?"

Wali Dad seemed to be in a very bad temper. Lalun looked out of the window and smiled into the dust-haze. I went away thinking about Khem Singh who had once made history with a thousand followers, and would have been a princeling but for the power of the supreme government.

The senior captain commanding Fort Amara was away on leave, but the subaltern, his deputy, had drifted down to the club, where I found him and inquired of him whether it was really true that a political prisoner had been added to the attractions of the fort. The subaltern explained at great length, for this was the first time that he had held command of the fort and his glory lay heavy upon him.

"Yes," said he, "a man was sent in to me about a week ago from down the line—a thorough gentleman whoever he is. Of course I did all I could for him. He had his two servants and some silver cooking-pots, and he looked for all the world like a native officer. I called him Subadar Sahib; just as well to be on the safe side, y'know. 'Look here, Subadar Sahib,' I said, 'you're handed over to my authority, and I'm supposed to guard you. Now I don't want to make your life hard, but you must make things easy for me. All the fort is at your disposal, from the flagstaff to the dry ditch, and I shall be happy to entertain you in any way I can, but you mustn't take advantage of it. Give me your word that you won't try to escape, Subadar Sahib, and I'll give you my word that you shall have no heavy guard put over you.' I thought the best way of getting at him was by going at him straight, y'know; and it was, by Jove! The old man gave me his word, and moved about the fort as contented as a sick crow. He's a rummy chap—always asking to be told where he is and what the buildings about him are. I had to sign a slip of blue paper when he turned up, acknowledging receipt of his body and all that, and I'm responsible, y'know, that he doesn't get away. Queer thing, though, looking after a Johnnie old enough to be your grandfather, isn't it? Come to the fort some day and see him."

For reasons which will appear, I never went to the fort while Khem Singh was then within its walls. I knew him only as a gray head seen from Lalun's window—a gray head and a harsh voice.

But natives told me that, day by day, as he looked upon the fair lands round Amara, his memory came back to him and, with it, the old hatred against the government that had been nearly effaced in far-off Burmah. So he raged up and down the west face of the fort from morning till noon and from evening till the night, devising vain things in his heart and croaking war-songs when Lalun sung on the city walls. As he grew more acquainted with the subaltern he unburdened his old heart of some of the passions that had withered it. "Sahib," he used to say, tapping his stick against the parapet, "when I was a young man I was one of twenty thousand horsemen who came out of the city and rode round the plain here. Sahib, I was the leader of a hundred, then of a thousand, then of five thousand, and now!"—he pointed to his two servants. "But from the beginning to to-day I would cut the throats of all the sahibs in the land if I could. Hold me fast, sahib, lest I get away and return to those who would follow me. I forgot them when I was in Burmah, but now that I am in my own country again, I remember everything."

"Do you remember that you have given me your honor not to make your tendance a hard matter?" said the subaltern.

"Yes, to you, only to you, sahib," said Khem Singh. "To you because you are of a pleasant countenance. If my turn comes again, sahib, I will not hang you nor cut your throat."

"Thank you," said the subaltern, gravely, as he looked along the line of guns that could pound the city to powder in half an hour. "Let us go into our own quarters, Khem Singh. Come and talk with me after dinner."

Khem Singh would sit on his own cushion at the subaltern's feet, drinking heavy, scented anise-seed brandy in great gulps, and telling strange stories of Fort Amara, which had been a palace, in the old days, of begums and ranees tortured to death—ay, in the very vaulted chamber that now served as a mess-room; would tell stories of Sobraon that made the subaltern's cheeks flush and tingle with pride of race, and of the Kuka rising from which so much was expected and the foreknowledge of which was shared by a hundred thousand souls. But he never told tales of '57 because, as he said, he was the subaltern's guest, and '57 is a year that no man, black or white, cares to speak of. Once only, when the anise-seed brandy had slightly affected his head, he said: "Sahib, speaking now of a matter which lay between Sobraon and the affair of the Kukas, it was ever a wonder to us that you stayed your hand at all, and that, having stayed it, you did not make the land one prison. Now I hear from without that you do great honor to all men of our country and by your own hands are destroying the terror of your name which is your strong rock and defense. This is a foolish thing. Will oil and water mix? Now in '57—"

"I was not born then, Subadar Sahib," said the subaltern, and Khem Singh reeled to his quarters.

The subaltern would tell me of these conversations at the club, and my desire to see Khem Singh increased. But Wali Dad, sitting in the window-seat of the house on the city wall, said it would be a cruel thing to do, and Lalun pretended that I preferred the society of a grizzled old Sikh to hers.

"Here is tobacco, here is talk, here are many friends and all the news of the city, and, above all, here is myself. I will tell you stories and sing you songs, and Wali Dad will talk his English nonsense in your ears. Is that worse than watching the caged animal yonder? Go to-morrow then, if you must, but to-day such and such a one will be here; he will speak of wonderful things."

It happened that to-morrow never came, and the warm heat of the latter rains gave place to the chill of early October almost before I was aware of the flight of the year. The captain commanding the fort returned from leave and took charge of Khem Singh according to the laws of the seniority. The captain was not a nice man. He called all natives "niggers," which, besides being extreme bad form, shows gross ignorance.

"What's the use of telling off two Tommies to watch that old nigger?" said he.

"I fancy it soothes his vanity," said the subaltern. "The men are ordered to keep well out of his way, but he takes them as a tribute to his importance, poor old beast."

"I won't have line men taken off regular guards in this way. Put on a couple of native infantry."

"Sikhs?" said the subaltern, lifting his brows.

"Sikhs, Pathans, Dogras—they're all alike, these black vermin," and the captain talked to Khem Singh in a manner which hurt that old gentleman's feelings. Fifteen years before, when he had been caught for the second time, every one looked upon him as a sort of tiger. He liked being regarded in this light. But he forgot that the world goes forward in fifteen years, and many subalterns are promoted to captaincies.

"The captain-pig is in charge of the fort?" said Khem Singh to his native guard every morning. And the native guard said: "Yes, Subadar Sahib," in deference to his age and his air of distinction; but they did not know who he was.

In those days the gathering in Lalun's little white room was always large and talked more mightily than before.

"The Greeks," said Wali Dad who had been borrowing my books, "the inhabitants of the city of Athens, where they were always hearing and telling some new thing, rigorously secluded their women—who were mostly fools. Hence the glorious institution of the heterodox women—is it not?—who were amusing and not fools. All the Greek philosophers delighted in their company. Tell me, my friend, how it goes now in Greece and the other places upon the Continent of Europe. Are your women-folk also fools?"

"Wali Dad," I said, "you never speak to us about your women-folk and we never speak about ours to you. That is the bar between us."

"Yes," said Wali Dad, "it is curious to think that our common meeting-place should be here, in the house of a common—how do you call her?" He pointed with the pipe-mouth to Lalun.

"Lalun is nothing else but Lalun," I said, and that was perfectly true. "But if you took your place in the world, Wali Dad, and gave up dreaming dreams—"

"I might wear an English coat and trousers. I might be a leading Mohammedan pleader. I might even be received at the commissioner's tennis-parties where the English stand on one side and the natives on the other, in order to promote social intercourse throughout the empire. Heart's heart," said he to Lalun, quickly, "the sahib says that I ought to quit you."

"The sahib is always talking stupid talk," returned Lalun with a laugh. "In this house I am a queen and thou art a king. The sahib"—she put her arms above her head and thought for a moment—"the sahib shall be our vizier—thine and mine, Wali Dad, because he has said that thou shouldst leave me."

Wali Dad laughed immoderately, and I laughed too. "Be it so," said he. "My friend, are you willing to take this lucrative government appointment? Lalun, what shall his pay be?"

But Lalun began to sing, and for the rest of

the time there was no hope of getting a sensible answer from her or Wali Dad. When the one stopped, the other began to quote Persian poetry with a triple pun in every other line. Some of it was not strictly proper, but it was all very funny, and it only came to an end when a fat person in black, with gold *pince-nez,* sent up his name to Lalun, and Wali Dad dragged me into the twinkling night to walk in a big rose garden and talk heresies about religion and governments and a man's career in life.

The Mohurrum, the great mourning festival of the Mohammedans, was close at hand, and the things that Wali Dad said about religious fanaticism would have secured his expulsion from the loosest-thinking Moslem sect. There were the rose bushes round us, the stars above us, and from every quarter of the city came the boom of the big Mohurrum drums. You must know that the city is divided in fairly equal proportions between the Hindoos and the Mussulmans, and when both creeds belong to the fighting races, a big religious festival gives ample chance for trouble. When they can—that is to say when the authorities are weak enough to allow it—the Hindoos do their best to arrange some minor feast-day of their own in time to clash with the period of general mourning for the martyrs Hasan and Hussain, the heroes of the Mohurrum. Gilt and painted paper presentations of their tombs are borne with shouting and wailing, music, torches and yells, through the principal thoroughfares of the city; which fakements are called *tazias*. Their passage is rigorously laid down beforehand by the police, and detachments of police accompany each *tazia*, lest the Hindoos should throw bricks at it and the peace of the queen and the heads of her loyal subjects should thereby be broken. Mohurrum time in a "fighting" town means anxiety to all the officials, because, if a riot breaks out, the officials and not the rioters are held responsible. The former must foresee everything, and while not making their precautions ridiculously elaborate, must see that they are at least adequate.

"Listen to the drums!" said Wali Dad. "That is the heart of the people—empty and making much noise. How, think you, will the Mohurrum go this year? I think that there will be trouble."

He turned down a side-street and left me alone with the stars and a sleepy police patrol. Then I went to bed and dreamed that Wali Dad had sacked the city and I was made vizier, with Lalun's silver *huqa* for mark of office.

All day the Mohurrum drums beat in the city, and all day deputations of tearful Hindoo gentlemen besieged the deputy commissioner with assurances that they would be murdered ere next dawning by the Mohammedans. "Which," said the deputy commissioner, in confidence to the head of police, "is a pretty fair indication that the Hindoos are going to make 'emselves unpleasant. I think we can arrange a little surprise for them.

I have given the heads of both creeds fair warning. If they choose to disregard it, so much the worse for them."

There was a large gathering in Lalun's house that night, but of men that I had never seen before, if I except the fat gentleman in black with the gold *pince-nez*. Wali Dad lay in the window-seat, more bitterly scornful of his faith and its manifestations than I had ever known him. Lalun's maid was very busy cutting up and mixing tobacco for the guests. We could hear the thunder of the drums as the processions accompanying each *tazia* marched to the central gathering place in the plain outside the city, preparatory to their triumphant re-entry and circuit within the walls. All the streets seemed ablaze with torches, and only Fort Amara was black and silent.

When the noise of the drums ceased, no one in the white room spoke for a time. "The first *tazia* has moved off," said Wali Dad, looking to the plain.

"That is very early," said the man with the *pince-nez*. "It is only half past eight." The company rose and departed.

"Some of them were men from Ladakh," said Lalun, when the last had gone. "They brought me brick-tea such as the Russians sell, and a tea-urn from Peshawur. Show me, now, how the English memsahibs make tea."

The brick-tea was abominable. When it was finished Wali Dad suggested a descent into the streets. "I am nearly sure that there will be trouble to-night," he said. "All the city thinks so, and *Vox Populi* is *Vox Dei,* as the Babus say. Now I tell you that at the corner of the Padshahi Gate you will find my horse all this night if you want to go about and see things. It is a most disgraceful exhibition. Where is the pleasure of saying '*Ya Hasan, Ya Hussain*' twenty thousand times in a night?"

All the professions—there were two-and-twenty of them—were now well within the city walls. The drums were beating afresh, the crowd were howling *"Ya Hasan! Ya Hussain!"* and beating their breasts, the brass bands were playing their loudest, and at every corner where space allowed Mohammedan preachers were telling the lamentable story of the death of the martyrs. It was impossible to move except with the crowd, for the streets were not more than twenty feet wide. In the Hindoo quarters the shutters of all the shops were up and cross-barred. As the first *tazia,* a gorgeous erection ten feet high, was borne aloft on the shoulders of a score of stout men into the semi-darkness of the gully of horsemen, a brickbat crashed through its talc and tinsel sides.

"Into Thy hands, oh, Lord!" murmured Wali Dad, profanely, as a yell went up from behind, and a native officer of police jammed his horse through the crowd. Another brickbat followed, and the *tazia* staggered and swayed where it had stopped.

"Go on! In the name of the Sirkar, go forward!" shouted the policemen, but there was an ugly cracking and splintering of shutters, and the crowd halted, with oaths and growlings, before the house whence the brickbat had been thrown.

Then, without any warning, broke the storm—not only in the gully of the horsemen, but in half a dozen other places. The *tazias* rocked like ships at sea, the long pole-torches dipped and rose round them while the men shouted: "The Hindoos are dishonoring the *tazias!* Strike! Strike! Into their temples for the faith!" The six or eight policemen with each *tazia* drew their batons, and struck as long as they could in the hope of forcing the mob forward, but they were overpowered, and as contingents of Hindoos poured into the streets, the fight became general. Half a mile away where the *tazias* were yet untouched the drums and the shrieks of *"Ya Hasan! Ya Hussain!"* continued, but not for long. The priests at the corners of the streets knocked the legs from the bedsteads that supported their pulpits and smote for the faith, while stones fell from the silent houses upon friend and foe, and the packed streets bellowed: *"Din! Din! Din!"* A *tazia* caught fire, and was dropped for a flaming barrier between Hindoo and Mussulman at the corner of the gully. Then the crowd surged forward, and Wali Dad drew me close to the stone pillar of a well.

"It was intended from the beginning!" he

shouted in my ear, with more heat than blank un-
belief should be guilty of. "The bricks were
carried up to the houses beforehand. These swine
of Hindoos! We shall be gutting kine in their
temples to-night!"

Tazia after *tazia,* some burning, others torn
to pieces, hurried past us and the mob with them,
howling, shrieking, and striking at the house
doors in their flight. At last we saw the reason
of the rush. Hugonin, the assistant district superintendent of police, a boy of twenty, had got
together thirty constables and was forcing the
crowd through the streets. His old gray police-
horse showed no sign of uneasiness as it was
spurred breast-on into the crowd, and the long
dog-whip with which he had armed himself was
never still.

"They know we haven't enough police to hold
'em," he cried as he passed me, mopping a cut on
his face. "They know we haven't! Aren't any
of the men from the club coming down to help?
Get on, you sons of burned fathers!" the dog-
whip cracked afresh across the writhing backs,
and the constables smote afresh with baton and
gun-butt. With these passed the lights and the
shouting, and Wali Dad began to swear under his
breath. From Fort Amara shot up a single
rocket; then two side by side. It was the signal
for troops.

Pettit, the deputy commissioner, covered with
dust and sweat, but calm and gently smiling, can-

tered up the clean-swept street in the rear of the main body of the rioters. "No one killed yet," he shouted. "I'll keep 'em on the run till dawn! Don't let 'em halt, Hugonin! Trot 'em about till the troops come."

The science of the defense lay solely in keeping the mob on the move. If they had breathing-space they would halt and fire a house, and then the work of restoring order would be more difficult, to say the least of it. Flames have the same effect on a crowd as blood has on a wild beast.

Word had reached the club and men in evening-dress were beginning to show themselves and lend a hand in heading off and breaking up the shouting masses with stirrup-leathers, whips, or chance-found staves. They were not very often attacked, for the rioters had sense enough to know that the death of a European would not mean one hanging but many, and possibly the appearance of the thrice-dreaded artillery. The clamor in the city redoubled. The Hindoos had descended into the streets in real earnest and ere long the mob returned. It was a strange sight. There were no *tazias*—only their riven platforms—and there were no police. Here and there a city dignitary, Hindoo or Mohammedan, was vainly imploring his coreligionists to keep quiet and behave themselves—advice for which his white beard was pulled with contumely. Then a native officer of police, unhorsed but still using his spurs with effect, would be seen borne along in the throng, warning all the world of the danger of insulting the government. Everywhere were men striking aimlessly with sticks, grasping each other by the throat, howling and foaming with rage, or beating with their bare hands on the doors of the houses.

"It is a lucky thing that they are fighting with natural weapons," I said to Wali Dad, "else we should have half the city killed."

I turned as I spoke and looked at his face. His nostrils were distended, his eyes were fixed, and he was smiting himself softly on the breast. The crowd poured by with renewed riot—a gang of Mussulmans hard-pressed by some hundred Hindoo fanatics. Wali Dad left my side with an oath, and shouting: *"Ya Hasan! Ya Hussain!"* plunged into the thick of the fight where I lost sight of him.

I fled by a side alley to the Padshahi Gate where I found Wali Dad's house, and thence rode to the fort. Once outside the city wall, the tumult sunk to a dull roar, very impressive under the stars and reflecting great credit on the fifty thousand able-bodied men who were making it. The troops who, at the deputy commissioner's instance, had been ordered to rendezvous quietly near the fort, showed no signs of being impressed. Two companies of native infantry and a squadron of native cavalry and a company of British infantry were kicking their heels in the shadow of the east face, waiting for orders to march in. I am sorry to say that they were all pleased, unholily pleased, at the chance of what they called "a little fun." The senior officers, to be sure, grumbled at having been kept out of bed, and the English troops pretended to be sulky, but there was joy in the hearts of all the subalterns, and whispers ran up and down the line: "No ball cartridge—what a beastly shame!" "D'you think the beggars will really stand up to us?" "Hope I shall meet my money-lender there. I owe him more than I can afford." "Oh, they won't let us even unsheath swords." "Hurrah! Up goes the fourth rocket. Fall in, there!"

The garrison artillery, who to the last cherished a wild hope that they might be allowed to bombard the city at a hundred yards' range, lined the parapet above the east gateway and cheered themselves hoarse as the British infantry doubled along the road to the main gate of the city. The cavalry cantered on to the Padshahi Gate, and the native infantry marched slowly to the Gate of the Butchers. The surprise was intended to be of a distinctly unpleasant nature, and to come on top of the defeat of the police who had been just able to keep the Mohammedans from firing the houses of a few leading Hindoos. The bulk of the riot lay in the north and northwest wards. The east and southeast were by this time dark and silent, and I rode hastily to Lalun's house, for I wished to tell her to send some one in search of Wali Dad. The house was unlighted, but the door

was open, and I climbed upstairs in the darkness.
One small lamp in the white room showed Lalun
and her maid leaning half out of the window,
breathing heavily and evidently pulling at something that refused to come.

"Thou art late—very late," gasped Lalun without turning her head. "Help us now, oh, fool,
if thou hast not spent thy strength howling
among the tazias. Pull! Nasiban and I can do
no more! Oh, sahib, is it you? The Hindoos
have been hunting an old Mohammedan round
the ditch with clubs. If they find him again they
will kill him. Help us to pull him up."

I laid my hands to the long red silk waist-cloth
that was hanging out of the window, and we
three pulled and pulled with all the strength at
our command. There was something very heavy
at the end, and it was swearing in an unknown
tongue as it kicked against the city wall.

"Pull, oh, pull!" said Lalun at the last. A pair
of brown hands grasped the window-sill and a
venerable Mohammedan tumbled upon the floor,
very much out of breath. His jaws were tied
up, and his turban had fallen over one eye. He
was dusty and angry.

Lalun hid her face in her hands for an instant
and said something about Wali Dad that I could
not catch.

Then, to my extreme gratification, she threw
her arms round my neck and murmured pretty
things. I was in no haste to stop her; and Nasi-

ban, being a hand-maiden of tact, turned to the
big jewel-chest that stands in the corner of the
white room and rummaged among the contents.
The Mohammedan sat on the floor and glared.

"One service more, sahib, since thou hast come
so opportunely," said Lalun. "Wilt thou"—it is
very nice to be thou-ed by Lalun—"take this old
man across the city—the troops are everywhere,
and they might hurt him, for he is old—to the
Kumharsen Gate? There I think he may find a
carriage to take him to his house. He is a friend
of mine, and thou art—more than a friend
. . . therefore I ask this."

Nasiban bent over the old man, tucked something into his belt, and I raised him up, and led
him into the streets. In crossing from the east to
the west of the city there was no chance of avoid-
ing the troops and the crowds. Long before I
reached the gully of horsemen I heard the shouts
of the British infantry crying cheerily: "Hutt,
ye beggars! Hutt, ye devils! Get along! Go
forward, there!" Then followed the ringing of
rifle-butts and shrieks of pain. The troops were
banging at the bare toes of the mob with their
butts—not a bayonet had been fixed. My companion mumbled and jabbered as we walked on
until we were carried back by the crowd and had
to force our way to the troops. I caught him by
the wrist and felt a bangle thereon—the iron
bangle of the Sikhs—but I had no suspicions, for
Lalun had only ten minutes before put her arms

around me. Thrice we were carried back by the crowd, and when we won our way past the British infantry it was to meet the Sikh cavalry driving another mob before them with the butts of their lances.

"What are these dogs?" said the old man.

"Sikhs of the cavalry, father," I said, and we edged our way up the line of horses two abreast and found the deputy commissioner, his helmet smashed on his head, surrounded by a knot of men who had come down from the club as amateur constables and had helped the police mightily.

"We'll put 'em on the run till dawn," said Pettit. "Who's your villainous friend?"

I had only time to say, "The protection of the Sirkar!" when a fresh crowd flying before the native infantry carried us a hundred yards nearer to the Kumharsen Gate, and Pettit was swept away like a shadow.

"I do not know—I can not see—it is all new to me!" moaned my companion. "How many troops are there in the city?"

"Perhaps five hundred," I said.

"A lakh of men beaten by five hundred—and Sikhs among them! Surely, surely, I am an old man, but—the Kumharsen Gate is new. Who pulled down the stone lions? Where is the conduit? Sahib, I am a very old man, and, alas, I— I can not stand." He dropped in the shadow of the Kumharsen Gate where there was no disturbance. A fat gentleman wearing gold *pince-nez* came out of the darkness.

"You are most kind to bring my old friend," he said, suavely. "He is a landholder of Akala. He should not be in a big city when there is religious excitement. But I have a carriage here. You are quite truly kind. Will you help me to put him into the carriage? It is very late."

We bundled the old man into a hired victoria that stood close to the gate, and I turned back to the house on the city wall. The troops were driving the people to and fro, while the police shouted, "To your houses! Get to your houses!" and the dog-whip of the assistant district superintendent cracked remorselessly. Terror-stricken *bunnias* clung to the stirrups of the cavalry, crying that their houses had been robbed (which was a lie), and the burly Sikh horsemen patted them on the shoulder and bade them return to those houses lest a worse thing should happen. Parties of five or six British soldiers, joining arms, swept down the side-gullies, their rifles on their backs, stamping, with shouting and song, upon the toes of Hindoo and Mussulman. Never was religious enthusiasm more systematically squashed; and never were poor breakers of the peace more utterly weary and foot-sore. They were routed out of holes and corners, from behind well-pillars and byres, and bidden to go to their houses. If they had no houses to go to, so much the worse for their toes.

On returning to Lalun's door I stumbled over a man at the threshold. He was sobbing hysterically and his arms flapped like the wings of a goose. It was Wali Dad, agnostic and unbeliever, shoeless, turbanless, and frothing at the mouth, the flesh on his chest bruised and bleeding from the vehemence with which he had smitten himself. A broken torch-handle lay by his side, and his quivering lips murmured, *"Ya Hasan! Ya Hussain!"* as I stooped over him. I pushed him a few steps up the staircase, threw a pebble at Lalun's city window, and hurried home.

Most of the streets were very still, and the cold wind that comes before the dawn whistled down them. In the center of the square of the mosque a man was bending over a corpse. The skull had been smashed in by gun butt or bamboo stave.

"It is expedient that one man should die for the people," said Pettit, grimly, raising the shapeless head. "These brutes were beginning to show their teeth too much."

And from afar we could hear the soldiers singing:

"Two Lovely Black Eyes," as they drove the remnant of the rioters within doors.

*   *   *   *   *   *

Of course you can guess what happened? I was not so clever. When the news went abroad

that Khem Singh had escaped from the fort, I
did not, since I was then living the story, not
writing it, connect myself, or Lalun, or the fat
gentleman of the gold *pince-nez,* with his disap-
pearance.   Nor did it strike me that Wali Dad
was the man who should have steered him across
the city, or that Lalun's arms round my neck were
put there to hide the money that Nasiban gave
to him, and then Lalun had used me and my white
face as even a better safeguard than Wali Dad,
who proved himself so untrustworthy.   All that
I knew at that time was that, when Fort Amara
was taken up with the riots, Khem Singh profited
by the confusion to get away, and that his two
Sikh guards also escaped.

But later on I received full enlightenment; and
so did Khem Singh.   He fled to those who knew
him in the old days, but many of them were dead
and more were changed, and all knew something
of the wrath of the government.   He went to the
young men, but the glamour of his name had
passed away, and they were entering native regi-
ments or government offices, and Khem Singh
could give them neither pension, decorations, nor
influence—nothing but a glorious death with their
backs to the mouth of a gun.   He wrote letters
and made promises, and the letters fell into bad
hands, and a wholly insignificant subordinate
officer of police tracked them down and gained
promotion thereby.   Moreover, Khem Singh was
old, and aniseed brandy was scarce, and he had

left his silver cooking-pots in Fort Amara with his nice warm bedding, and the gentleman with the gold *pince-nez* was told by those who had employed him that Khem Singh as a popular leader was not worth the money paid.

"Great is the mercy of these fools of English," said Khem Singh when the situation was explained. "I will go back to Fort Amara of my own free will and gain honor. Give me good clothes to return in."

So, upon a day, Khem Singh knocked at the wicket gate of the fort and walked to the captain and the subaltern who were nearly gray-headed on account of correspondence that daily arrived from Simla marked "Private."

"I have come back, Captain Sahib," said Khem Singh. "Put no more guards over me. It is no good out yonder."

A week later I saw him for the first time to my knowledge, and he made as though there were an understanding between us.

"It was well done, sahib," said he, "and greatly I admire your astuteness in thus boldly facing the troops when I, whom they would have doubtless torn to pieces, was with you. Now there is a man in Fort Ooltagarh whom a bold man could with ease help to escape. This is the position of the fort as I draw it on the sand . . ."

But I was thinking how I had become Lalun's vizier after all.

THE JUDGMENT OF DUNGARA

SEE the pale martyr with his shirt on fire.—*Printer's Error*.

THEY tell the tale even now among the *sâl* groves of the Berbulda Hill, and for corroboration point to the roofless and windowless mission-house. The great God Dungara, the God of Things as They Are, most terrible, one-eyed, bearing the red elephant tusk, did it all; and he who refuses to believe in Dungara will assuredly be smitten by the madness of Yat—the madness that fell upon the sons and the daughters of the Buria Kol when they turned aside from Dungara and put on clothes. So says Athon Dazé, who is High Priest of the Shrine and Warden of the Red Elephant tusk. But if you ask the assistant collector and agent in charge of the Buria Kol, he will laugh—not because he bears any malice against missions, but because he himself saw the vengeance of Dungara executed upon the spiritual children of the Rev. Justus Krenk, pastor of the Turbingen Mission, and upon Lotta, his virtuous wife.

Yet if ever a man merited good treatment of the gods it was the Reverend Justus, one time of Heidelberg, who, on the faith of a call, went into the wilderness and took the blonde, blue-eyed

Lotta with him. "We will these heathen now by idolatrous practices so darkened better make," said Justus in the early days of his career. "Yes," he added, with conviction, "they shall be good and shall with their hands to work learn. For all good Christians must work." And upon a stipend more modest even than that of an English lay-reader, Justus Krenk kept house beyond Kamala and the gorge of Malair, beyond the Berbulda River close to the foot of the blue hill of Panth, on whose summit stands the Temple of Dungara—in the heart of the country of the Buria Kol—the naked, good-tempered, timid, shameless, lazy Buria Kol.

Do you know what life at a mission outpost means? Try to imagine a loneliness exceeding that of the smallest station to which government has ever sent you—isolation that weighs upon the waking eyelids and drives you perforce headlong into the labors of the day. There is no post, there is no one of your own color to speak to, there are no roads: there is, indeed, food to keep you alive, but it is not pleasant to eat; and whatever of good or beauty or interest there is in your life, must come from yourself and the grace that may be planted in you.

In the morning, with a patter of soft feet, the converts, the doubtful, and the open scoffers, troop up to the veranda. You must be infinitely kind and patient, and, above all, clear-sighted, for you deal with the simplicity of childhood, the experience of man, and the subtlety of the savage. Your congregation have a hundred material wants to be considered; and it is for you, as you believe in your personal responsibility to your Maker, to pick out of the clamoring crowd any grain of spirituality that may lie therein. If to the cure of souls you add that of bodies, your task will be all the more difficult, for the sick and the maimed will profess any and every creed for the sake of healing, and will laugh at you because you are simple enough to believe them.

As the day wears and the impetus of the morning dies away, there will come upon you an overwhelming sense of the uselessness of your toil. This must be striven against, and the only spur in your side will be the belief that you are playing against the devil for the living soul. It is a great, a joyous belief; but he who can hold it unwavering for four-and-twenty consecutive hours must be blessed with an abundantly strong physique and equable nerve.

Ask the gray heads of the Bannockburn Medical Crusade what manner of life their preachers lead; speak to the Racine Gospel Agency, those lean Americans whose boast is that they go where no Englishman dare follow; get a pastor of the Tubingen Mission to talk of his experiences—if you can. You will be referred to the printed reports, but these contain no mention of the men who have lost youth and health, all that a man may lose except faith, in the wilds; of English maidens who have gone forth and died in the fever-stricken jungle of the Panth Hills, knowing from the first that death was almost a certainty. Few pastors will tell you of these things any more than they will speak of that young David of St. Bees, who, set apart for the Lord's work, broke down in the utter desolation, and returned half distraught to the head mission crying: "There is no God, but I have walked with the devil!"

The reports are silent here, because heroism, failure, doubt, despair and self-abnegation on the part of a mere cultured white man are things of no weight as compared to the saving of one half-human soul from a fantastic faith in wood-spirits, goblins of the rock, and river-fiends.

And Gallio, the assistant collector of the country-side, "cared for none of these things." He had been long in the district, and the Buria Kol loved him and brought him offerings of speared fish, orchids from the dim moist heart of the forests, and as much game as he could eat. In return, he gave them quinine, and with Athon Dazé, the high priest, controlled their simple policies.

"When you have been some years in the country," said Gallio at the Krenks' table, "you grow to find one creed as good as another. I'll give you all the assistance in my power, of course, but don't hurt my Buria Kol. They are a good people and they trust me."

"I will them the Word of the Lord teach," said Justus, his round face beaming with enthusiasm, "and I will assuredly to their prejudices no wrong hastily without thinking make. But, oh, my friend, this in the mind impartiality-of-creed-judgment-belooking is very bad."

"Heigh-ho!" said Gallio, "I have their bodies and the district to see to, but you can try what you can do for their souls. Only don't behave as your predecessor did, or I'm afraid that I can't guarantee your life."

"And that?" said Lotta, sturdily, handing him a cup of tea.

"He went up to the Temple of Dungara—to be sure he was new to the country—and began hammering old Dungara over the head with an umbrella; so the Buria Kol turned out and hammered him rather savagely. I was in the district, and he sent a runner to me with a note, saying: 'Persecuted for the Lord's sake. Send wing of regiment.' The nearest troops were about two hundred miles off, but I guessed what he had been doing. I rode to Panth and talked to old Athon Dazé like a father, telling him that a man of his wisdom ought to have known that the sahib had sunstroke and was mad. You never saw a people more sorry in your life. Athon Dazé apologized, sent wood and milk and fowls and all sorts of things; and I gave five rupees to the shrine and told Macnamara that he had been injudicious. He said that I had bowed down in the House of

Rimmon; but if he had only just gone over the brow of the hill and insulted Palin Deo, the idol of the Suria Kol, he would have been impaled on a charred bamboo long before I could have done anything, and then I should have had to have hanged some of the poor brutes. Be gentle with them, padri—but I don't think you'll do much."

"Not I," said Justus, "but my Master. We will with the little children begin. Many of them will be sick—that is so. After the children the mothers; then the men. But I would greatly that you were in internal sympathies with us prefer."

Gallio departed to risk his life in mending the rotten bamboo bridges of his people, in killing a too-persistent tiger here or there, in sleeping out in the reeking jungle, or in tracking the Suria Kol raiders who had taken a few heads from their brethren of the Buria clan. A knock-kneed, shambling young man was Gallio, naturally devoid of creed or reverence, with a longing for absolute power which his undesirable district gratified.

"No one wants my post," he used to say grimly, "and my collector only pokes his nose in when he's quite certain there is no fever. I'm monarch of all I survey, and Athon Dazé is my viceroy."

Because Gallio prided himself on his supreme disregard of human life—though he never extended the theory beyond his own—he naturally rode forty miles to the mission with a tiny brown baby on his saddle-bow.

"Here is something for you, padri," said he. "The Kols leave their surplus children to die. Don't see why they shouldn't, but you may rear this one. I picked it up beyond the Berbulda fork. I've a notion that the mother has been following me through the woods ever since."

"It is the first of the fold," said Justus, and Lotta caught up the screaming morsel to her bosom and hushed it craftily; while, as a wolf hangs in the field, Matui, who had borne it and in accordance with the law of her tribe had exposed it to die, panted wearily and foot-sore in the bamboo brake, watching the house with hungry mother-eyes. What should the omnipotent assistant collector do? Would the little man in the black coat eat her daughter alive as Athon Dazé said was the custom of all men in black coats?

Matui waited among the bamboos through the long night; and, in the morning, there came forth a fair white woman, the like of whom Matui had never seen, and in her arms was Matui's daughter clad in spotless raiment. Lotta knew little of the tongue of the Buria Kol, but when mother calls to mother, speech is easy to understand. By the hands stretched timidly to the hem of her gown, by the passionate gutturals and the longing eyes, Lotto understood with whom she had to deal. So Matui took the child again—would be a servant, even a slave, to this wonderful white woman, for her own tribe would recognize her no more. And Lotta wept over her exhaustively, after the German fashion, which includes much blowing of the nose.

"First the child, then the mother, and last the man, and the glory of God all," said Justus the Hopeful. And the man came, with a bow and arrows, very angry indeed, for there was no one to cook for him.

But the tale of the mission is a long one, and I have no space to show how Justus, forgetful of his injudicious predecessor, grievously smote Moto, the husband of Matui, for his brutality; how Moto was startled, but being released from the fear of instant death, took heart and became the faithful ally and first convert to Justus; how the little gathering grew, to the huge disgust of Athon Dazé; how the priest of the God of Things as They Are argued subtlely with the priest of the God of Things as They Should Be, and was worsted; how the dues of the Temple of Dungara fell away in fowls and fish and honeycomb; how Lotta lightened the curse of Eve among the women, and how Justus did his best to introduce the curse of Adam; how the Buria Kol rebelled at this, saying that their god was an idle god, and how Justus partially overcame their scruples against work, and taught them that the black earth was rich in other produce than pig-nuts only.

All these things belong to the history of many months, and throughout those months the white-

haired Athon Dazé meditated revenge for the
tribal neglect of Dungara. With savage cunning he feigned friendship toward Justus, even
hinting at his own conversion; but to the congregation of Dungara he said, darkly: "They of
the padri's flock have put on clothes and worship
a busy God. Therefore Dungara will afflict them
grievously till they throw themselves howling into
the waters of the Berbulda." At night the Red
Elephant Tusk boomed and groaned among the
hills, and the faithful waked and said: "The
God of Things as They Are matures revenge
against the backsliders. Be merciful, Dungara,
to us thy children, and give us all their crops!"

Late in the cold weather the collector and his
wife came into the Buria Kol country. "Go and
look at Krenk's mission," said Gallio. "He is doing good work in his own way, and I think he'd
be pleased if you opened the bamboo chapel that
he has managed to run up. At any rate, you'll
see a civilized Buria Kol."

Great was the stir in the mission. "Now he
and the gracious lady will that we have done good
work with their own eyes see, and—yes—we will
him our converts in all their new clothes by their
own hands constructed exhibit. It will a great
day be—for the Lord always," said Justus; and
Lotta said "Amen."

Justus had, in his quiet way, felt jealous of the
Basel Weaving Mission, his own converts being
unhandy; but Athon Dazé had latterly induced

some of them to hackle the glossy silky fibers of a plant that grew plenteously on the Panth Hill. It yielded a cloth white and smooth almost as the *tappa* of the South Seas, and that day the converts were to wear for the first time clothes made therefrom. Justus was proud of his work.

"They shall in white clothes clothed to meet the collector and his well-born lady come down, singing, 'Now thank we all our God.' Then he will the chapel open, and—yes—even Gallio to believe will begin. Stand so, my children, two by two, and—Lotta, why do they thus themselves scratch? It is not seemly to wriggle, Nala, my child. The collector will be here and be pained."

The collector, his wife, and Gallio climbed the hill to the mission station. The converts were drawn up in two lines, a shining band nearly forty strong. "Hah!" said the collector, whose acquisitive bent of mind led him to believe that he had fostered the institution from the first.

"Advancing, I see, by leaps and bounds."

Never was truer word spoken! The mission was advancing exactly as he had said—at first by little hops and shuffles of shame-faced uneasiness, but soon by the leaps of fly-stung horses and the bounds of maddened kangaroos. From the hill of Panth the Red Elephant Tusk delivered a dry and anguished blare. The ranks of the converts wavered, broke and scattered with yells and shrieks of pain, while Justus and Lotta stood horror-stricken.

"It is the judgment of Dungara!" shouted a voice. "I burn! I burn! To the river or we die!"

The mob wheeled and headed for the rocks that overhung the Berbulda, writhing, stamping, twisting and shedding its garments as it ran, pursued by the thunder of the trumpet of Dungara. Justus and Lotta fled to the collector almost in tears.

"I can not understand! Yesterday," panted Justus, "they had the Ten Commandments— What is this? Praise the Lord all good spirits by land or by sea. Nala! Oh, shame!"

With a bound and a scream there alighted on the rocks above their heads, Nala, once the pride of the mission, a maiden of fourteen summers, good, docile, and virtuous—now naked as the dawn and spitting like a wild-cat.

"Was it for this!" she raved, hurling her petticoat at Justus; "was it for this I left my people and Dungara—for the fires of your bad place? Blind ape, little earthworm, dried fish that you are, you said that I should never burn! Oh, Dungara, I burn now! I burn now! Have mercy, God of Things as They Are!"

She turned and flung herself into the Berbulda, and the trumpet of Dungara bellowed jubilantly. The last of the converts of the Tubingen Mission had put a quarter of a mile of rapid river between herself and her teachers.

"Yesterday," gulped Justus, "she taught in the

school of A, B, C, D.   Oh! It is the work of
Satan!"

But Gallio was curiously regarding the maiden's
petticoat where it had fallen at his feet. He felt
its texture, drew back his shirt-sleeve beyond the
deep tan of his hand and pressed a fold of the
cloth against the flesh. A blotch of angry red
rose on the white skin.

"Ah!" said Gallio, calmly. "I thought so."

"What is it?" said Justus.

"I should call it the Shirt of Nessus, but—
Where did you get the fiber of this cloth from?"

"Athon Dazé," said Justus. "He showed the
boys how it should manufactured be."

"The old fox! Do you know that he has given
you the Nilgiri nettle—scorpion—*Girardenia
heterophylla*—to work up. No wonder they
squirmed! Why, it stings even when they make
bridge-ropes of it, unless it's soaked for six weeks.
The cunning brute! It would take about half an
hour to burn through their thick hides, and
then—!"

Gallio burst into laughter, but Lotta was weeping in the arms of the collector's wife, and Justus
had covered his face with his hands.

"*Girardenia heterophylla!*" repeated Gallio.
"Krenk, why didn't you tell me? I could have
saved you this. Woven fire! Anybody but a
naked Kol would have known it, and, if I'm a
judge of their ways, you'll never get them back."

He looked across the river to where the converts

were still wallowing and wailing in the shallows, and the laughter died out of his eyes, for he saw that the Tubingen Mission to the Buria Kol was dead.

Never again, though they hung mournfully round the deserted school for three months, could Lotta or Justus coax back even the most promising of their flock. No! The end of conversion was the fire of the bad place—fire that ran through the limbs and gnawed into the bones. Who dare a second time tempt the anger of Dungara? Let the little man and his wife go elsewhere. The Buria Kol would have none of them. An unofficial message to Athon Dazé that if a hair of their heads were touched, Athon Dazé and the priests of Dungara would be hanged by Gallio at the temple shrine, protected Justus and Lotta from the stumpy poisoned arrows of the Buria Kol, but neither fish nor fowl, honeycomb, salt, nor young pig were brought to their doors any more. And, alas! man cannot live by grace alone if meat be wanting.

"Let us go, mine wife," said Justus; "there is no good here, and the Lord has willed that some other man shall the work take—in good time—in His own good time. We will go away, and I will—yes—some botany bestudy."

If any one is anxious to convert the Buria Kol afresh, there lies at least the core of a mission-house under the hill of Panth. But the chapel and school have long since fallen back into jungle.

GEMINI

GREAT is the justice of the White Man—greater the power of a lie.—*Native Proverb.*

THIS is your English justice, protector of the poor. Look at my back and loins, which are beaten with sticks—heavy sticks! I am a poor man, and there is no justice in courts.

There were two of us, and we were born of one birth, but I swear to you that I was born the first, and Ram Dass is the younger by three full breaths. The astrologer said so, and it is written in my horoscope—the horoscope of Durga Dass.

But we were alike—I and my brother who is a beast without honor—so alike that none knew, together or apart, which was Durga Dass. I am a Mahajun of Pali in Marwar, and an honest man. This is true talk. When we were men, we left our father's house in Pali, and went to the Punjab, where all the people are mud-heads and sons of asses. We took shop together in Isser Jang—I and my brother—near the big well where the governor's camp draws water. But Ram Dass, who is without truth, made quarrel with me, and we were divided. He took his books, and his pots, and his Mark, and became a *bunnia*— a money-lender—in the long street of Isser Jang, near the gate-way of the road that goes to Montgomery. It was not my fault that we pulled each other's turbans. I am a Mahajun of Pali, and I always speak true talk. Ram Dass was the thief and the liar.

Now, no man, not even the little children, could at one glance see which was Ram Dass and which was Durga Dass. But all the people of Isser Jang—may they die without sons!—said that we were thieves. They used much bad talk, but I took money on their bedsteads and their cooking-pots and the standing crop and the calf unborn, from the well in the big square to the gate of the Montgomery road. They were fools, these people —unfit to cut the toe-nails of a Marwari from Pali. I lent money to them all. A little, very little only—here a pice and there a pice.

God is my witness that I am a poor man! The money is all with Ram Dass—may his sons turn Christian, and his daughter be a burning fire and a shame in the house from generation to generation! May she die unwed, and be the mother of a multitude of bastards! Let the light go out in the house of Ram Dass, my brother. This I pray daily twice—with offerings and charms. Thus the trouble began. We divided the town of Isser Jang between us—I and my brother. There was a landholder beyond the gates, living but one short mile out, on the road that leads to Montgomery, and his name was Mohammed Shah, son of a Nawab. He was a great devil and drank wine. So long as there were women in his house, and wine and money for the marriage-feasts, he was merry and wiped his mouth. Ram Dass lent him the money, a lakh or half a lakh—how do I know? —and so long as the money was lent, the land-holder cared not what he signed.

The people of Issar Jang were my portion, and the landholder and the out-town was the portion of Ram Dass; for so we had arranged. I was the poor man, for the people of Issar Jang were without wealth. I did what I could, but Ram Dass had only to wait without the door of the land-holder's garden-court, and to lend him the money; taking the bonds from the hands of the steward.

In the autumn of the year after the lending, Ram Dass said to the landholder: "Pay me my money;" but the landholder gave him abuse. But Ram Dass went into the courts with the papers and the bonds—all correct—and took out decrees against the landholder; and the name of the gov-ernment was across the stamps of the decrees. Ram Dass took field by field, and mango-tree by mango-tree, and well by well; putting in his own men—debtors of the out-town of Isser Jang—to cultivate the crops. So he crept up across the land, for he had the papers, and the name of the government was across the stamps, till his men held the crops for him on all sides of the big white house of the landholder. It was well done; but when the landholder saw these things he was very angry and cursed Ram Dass after the man-ner of the Mohammedans.

And thus the landholder was angry, but Ram Dass laughed and claimed more fields, as was written upon the bonds. This was in the month of Phagun. I took my horse and went out to speak to the man who makes lac-bangles upon the road that leads to Montgomery, because he owed me a debt. There was in front of me, upon his horse, my brother Ram Dass. And when he saw me, he turned aside into the high crops, because there was hatred between us. And I went forward till I came to the orange-bushes by the landholder's house. The bats were flying, and the evening smoke was low down upon the land. Here met me four men—swashbucklers and Mohammedans —with their faces bound up, laying hold of my horse's bridle and crying out: "This is Ram Dass! Beat!" Me they beat with their staves— heavy staves bound about with wire at the end, such weapons as those swine of Punjabis use— till, having cried for mercy, I fell down senseless. But these shameless ones still beat me, saying: "Oh, Ram Dass, this is your interest—well weighed and counted into your hand, Ram Dass." I cried aloud that I was not Ram Dass but Durga Dass, his brother, yet they only beat me the more, and when I could make no more outcry they left me. But I saw their faces. There was Elahi Baksh who runs by the side of the landholder's white horse, and Nur Ali the keeper of the door, and Wajib Ali the very strong cook, and Abdul Latif the messenger—all of the household of the

landholder. These things I can swear on the cow's
tail if need be, but—Ahi! Ahi!—it has been already sworn, and I am a poor man whose honor is
lost.

When these four had gone away laughing, my
brother Ram Dass came out of the crops and
mourned over me as one dead.   But I opened my
eyes, and prayed him to get me water.   When I
had drunk, he carried me on his back, and by
by-ways brought me into the town of Isser Jang.
My heart was turned to Ram Dass, my brother,
in that hour, because of his kindness, and I lost my
enmity.

But a snake is a snake till it is dead; and a
liar is a liar till the judgment of the gods takes
hold of his heel.   I was wrong in that I trusted
my brother—the son of my mother.

When we had come to his house and I was a
little restored, I told him my tale, and he said:
"Without doubt, it is me whom they would have
beaten.   But the law courts are open, and there is
the justice of the Sirkar above all; and to the law
courts do thou go when this sickness is overpast."

Now when we two had left Pali in the old
years, there fell a famine that ran from Jeysulmir
to Gurgaon and touched Gogunda in the south.
At that time the sister of my father came away
and lived with us in Isser Jang; for a man must
above all see that his folk do not die of want.
When the quarrel between us twain came about,

the sister of my father—a lean she-dog without teeth—said that Ram Dass had the right, and went with him.   Into her hands—because she knew medicines and many cures—Ram Dass, my brother, put me faint with the beating and much bruised even to the pouring of blood from the mouth.   When I had two days' sickness the fever came upon me; and I set aside the fever to the account written in my mind against the landholder.

The Punjabis of Isser Jang are all the sons of Belial and a she-ass, but they are very good witnesses, bearing testimony unshakenly whatever the pleaders may say.   I would purchase witnesses by the score, and each man should give evidence, not only against Nur Ali, Wajib Ali, Abdul Latif and Elahi Baksh, but against the landholder, saying that he upon his white horse had called his men to beat me; and, further, that they had robbed me of two hundred rupees.   For the latter testimony, I would remit a little of the debt of the man who sold the lac-bangles, and he should say that he had put the money into my hands, and had seen the robbery from afar, but, being afraid, had run away.   This plan I told to my brother Ram Dass; and he said that the arrangement was good, and bade me take comfort and make swift work to be abroad again.   My heart was open to my brother in my sickness, and I told him the names of those whom I would call as witnesses—all men in my debt, but of that the magistrate sahib could have no knowledge, nor the landholder.   The fever stayed with me, and after the fever, I was taken with colic, and gripings very terrible. In that day I thought that my end was at hand, but I know now that she who gave me the medicines, the sister of my father—a widow, with a widow's heart—had brought about my second sickness. Ram Dass, my brother, said that my house was shut and locked, and brought me the big door-key and my books, together with all the moneys that were in my house—even the money that was buried under the floor; for I was in great fear lest thieves should break in and dig. I speak true talk; there was but very little money in my house. Perhaps ten rupees—perhaps twenty. How can I tell? God's my witness that I am a poor man.

One night, when I had told Ram Dass all that was in my heart of the lawsuit that I would bring against the landholder, and Ram Dass said that he had made the arrangement with the witnesses, giving me their names written, I was taken with a new great sickness, and they put me on the bed. When I was a little recovered—I can not tell how many days afterward—I made inquiry for Ram Dass, and the sister of my father said that he had gone to Montgomery upon a lawsuit. I took medicine and slept very heavily without waking. When my eyes were opened, there was a great stillness in the house of Ram Dass, and none answered when I called—not even the sister of my father. This filled me with fear, for I knew not what had happened.

Taking a stick in my hand, I went out slowly, till I came to the great square by the well, and my heart was hot in me against the landholder because of the pain of every step I took.

I called for Jowar Singh, the carpenter, whose name was first upon the list of those who should bear evidence against the landholder, saying: "Are all things ready, and do you know what should be said?"

Jowar Singh answered: "What is this, and whence do you come, Durga Dass?"

I said: "From my bed, where I have so long lain sick because of the landholder. Where is Ram Dass, my brother, who was to have made the arrangements for the witnesses? Surely you and yours know these things?"

Then Jowar Singh said: "What has this to do with us, oh, liar? I have borne witness and have been paid, and the landholder has, by the order of the court, paid both the five hundred rupees that he robbed from Ram Dass and yet other five hundred because of the great injury he did to your brother."

The well and the jujube-tree above it and the square of Isser Jang became dark in my eyes, but I leaned on my stick and said: "Nay! This is child's talk and senseless. It was I who suffered at the hands of the landholder, and I am come to make ready the case. Where is my brother Ram Dass?"

But Jowar Singh shook his head, and a woman cried: "What lie is here? What quarrel had the landholder with you, *bunnia?* It is only a shameless one and one without faith who profits by his brother's smarts. Have these *bunnias* no bowels?"

I cried again, saying: "By the Cow—by the Oath of the Cow, by the Temple of the Blue-throated Mahadeo—I and I only was beaten—beaten to the death! Let our talk be straight, oh, people of Isser Jang, and I will pay for the witnesses." I tottered where I stood, for the sickness and the pain of the beating were heavy upon me.

Then Ram Narain, who has his carpet spread under the jujube-tree by the well, and writes all letters for the men of the town, came up and said: "To-day is the one-and-fortieth day since the beating, and since these six days the case has been judged in the court, and the assistant commissioner sahib has given it for your brother Ram Dass, allowing the robbery, to which, too, I bore witness, and all things else as the witnesses said. There were many witnesses, and twice Ram Dass became senseless in the court because of his wounds, and the Stunt Sahib—the *baba* Stunt Sahib—gave him a chair before all the pleaders. Why do you howl, Durga Dass? These things fell as I have said. Was it not so?"

And Jowar Singh said: "That is truth. I was there, and there was a red cushion in the chair."

And Ram Narain said: "Great shame has

come upon the landholder because of this judgment, and fearing his anger, Ram Dass and all his house have gone back to Pali. Ram Dass told us that you also had gone first, the enmity being healed between you, to open a shop in Pali. Indeed, it were well for you that you go even now, for the landholder has sworn that if he catch any one of your house, he will hang him by the heels from the well-beam, and, swinging him to and fro, will beat him with staves till the blood runs from his ears. What I have said in respect to the case is true as these men here can testify—even to the five hundred rupees."

I said: "Was it five hundred?" And Kirpa Ram, the *jat,* said: "Five hundred; for I bore witness also."

And I groaned, for it had been in my heart to have said two hundred only.

Then a new fear came upon me and my bowels turned to water, and, running swiftly to the house of Ram Dass, I sought for my books and my money in the great wooden chest under my bedstead. There remained nothing; not even a cowrie's value. All had been taken by the devil who said he was my brother. I went to my own house also and opened the boards of the shutters; but there also was nothing save the rats among the grain-baskets. In that hour my senses left me, and, tearing my clothes, I ran to the well-place, crying out for the justice of the English on my brother Ram Dass, and, in my madness, telling all that the books were lost. When men saw that I would have jumped down the well, they believed the truth of my talk; more especially because upon my back and bosom were still the marks of the staves of the landholder.

Jowar Singh the carpenter withstood me, and turning me in his hands—for he is a very strong man—showed the scars upon my body, and bowed down with laughter upon the well-curb. He cried aloud so that all heard him, from the well-square to the caravansary of the pilgrims: "Oho! The jackals have quarreled, and the gray one has been caught in the trap. In truth, this man has been grievously beaten, and his brother has taken the money which the court decreed! Oh, *bunnia,* this shall be told for years against you! The jackals have quarreled, and, moreover, the books are burned. Oh, people indebted to Durga Dass—and I know that ye be many—the books are burned!"

Then all Isser Jang took up the cry that the books were burned. *Ahi! Ahi!* that in my folly I had let that escape my mouth—and they laughed throughout the city. They gave me the abuse of the Punjabi, which is a terrible abuse and very *tez;* pelting me also with sticks and cow-dung till I fell down and cried for mercy.

Ram Narain, the letter-writer, bade the people cease, for fear that the news should get into Montgomery, and the policemen might come down to inquire. He said, using many bad words: "This much mercy will I do to you, Durga Dass, though there was no mercy in your dealings with my sister's son over the matter of the dun heifer. Has any man a pony on which he sets no store, that this fellow may escape? If the landholder hears that one of the twain (and God knows whether he beat one or both, but this man is certainly beaten) be in the city, there will be a murder done, and then will come the police, making inquisition into each man's house and eating the sweet-seller's stuff all day long."

Kirpa Ram, the *jat,* said: "I have a pony very sick. But with beating he can be made to walk for two miles. If he dies, the hide-seller's will have the body."

Then Chumbo, the hide-seller, said: "I will pay three annas for the body, and will walk by this man's side till such time as the pony dies. If it be more than two miles, I will pay two annas only."

Kirpa Ram said: "Be it so." Men brought out the pony, and I asked leave to draw water from the well, because I was dried up with fear.

Then Ram Narain said: "Here be four annas. God has brought you very low, Durga Dass, and I would not send you away empty, even though the matter of my sister's son's dun heifer be an open sore between us. It is a long way to your own country. Go, and if it be so willed, live; but, above all, do not take the pony's bridle, for that is mine."

And I went out of Isser Jang, amid the laughing of the huge-thighed *jats,* and the hide-seller walked by my side waiting for the pony to fall dead. In one mile it died, and being full of fear of the landholder, I ran till I could run no more and came to this place.

But I swear by the Cow, I swear by all things whereon Hindoos and Mussulmans, and even the sahibs swear, that I, and not my brother, was beaten by the landholder. But the case is shut and the doors of the law courts are shut, and God knows where the *baba* Stunt Sahib—the mother's milk is not dry upon his hairless lip—is gone. *Ahi! Ahi!* I have no witnesses, and the scars will heal, and I am a poor man. But, on my Father's Soul, on the oath of a Mahajun from Pali, I, and not my brother, was beaten by the landholder!

What can I do? The Justice of the English is as a great river. Having gone forward, it does not return. Howbeit, do you, Sahib, take a pen and write clearly what I have said, that the Dipty Sahib may see, and reprove the Stunt Sahib, who is a colt yet unlicked by the mare, so young is he. I, and not my brother, was beaten, and he is gone to the west—I do not know where.

But, above all things, write—so that Sahibs may read, and his disgrace be accomplished—that Ram Dass, my brother, son of Purun Dass, Mahajun of Pali, is a swine and a night-thief, a taker of life, an eater of flesh, jackal-spawn without beauty, or faith, or cleanliness, or honor!

IN FLOOD TIME

Tweed said tae Till:—
"What gars ye rin sae still?"
Till said tae Tweed:—
"Though ye rin wi' speed
    And I rin slaw—
Yet where ye droon ae man
    I droon twa."

THERE is no getting over the river to-night, sahib. They say that a bullock-cart has been washed down already, and the *ekka* that went over half an hour before you came has not yet reached the far side. Is the sahib in haste? I will drive the ford-elephant in to show him. *Ohe, mahout* there in the shed! Bring out Ram Pershad, and if he will face the current, good. An elephant never lies, sahib, and Ram Pershad is separated from his friend Kala Nag. He, too, wishes to cross to the far side. Well done! Well done! my king! Go half-way across, *mahoutji* and see what the river says. Well done, Ram Pershad! Pearl among elephants, go into the river! Hit him on the head, fool! Was the goad made only to scratch thy own fat back with, bastard? Strike! Strike! What are the bowlders to thee, Ram Pershad, my Rustum, my mountain of strength? Go in! Go in!

No, sahib! It is useless. You can hear him

trumpet. He is telling Kala Nag that he can not come over. See! He has swung round and is shaking his head. He is no fool. He knows what the Barhwi means when it is angry. Aha! Indeed, thou art no fool, my child! Salam, Ram Pershad, Bahadur! Take him under the trees, *mahout,* and see that he gets his spices. Well done, thou chiefest among tuskers. Salam to the sirkar and go to sleep.

What is to be done? The sahib must wait till the river goes down. It will shrink to-morrow morning, if God pleases, or the day after at the latest. Now why does the sahib get so angry? I am his servant. Before God, I did not create this stream! What can I do? My hut and all that is therein is at the service of the sahib, and it is beginning to rain. Come away, my lord. How will the river go down for your throwing abuse at it? In the old days the English people were not thus. The fire-carriage has made them soft. In the old days, when they drove behind horses by day or by night, they said naught if a river barred the way or a carriage sat down in the mud. It was the will of God—not like a fire-carriage which goes and goes and goes, and would go though all the devils in the land hung on to its tail. The fire-carriage hath spoiled the English people. After all, what is a day lost, or, for that matter, what are two days? Is the sahib going to his own wedding, that he is so mad with haste? Ho! Ho! Ho! I am an old man and see few sahibs. For-

give me if I have forgotten the respect that is
due to them. The sahib is not angry?

His own wedding! Ho! Ho! Ho! The mind
of an old man is like the numah-tree. Fruit, bud,
blossom, and the dead leaves of all the years of
the past flourish together. Old and new and that
which is gone out of remembrance, all three are
there! Sit on the bedstead, sahib, and drink
milk. Or—would the sahib in truth care to drink
my tobacco? It is good. It is the tobacco of
Nuklao. My son, who is in service there, sent it
to me. Drink, then, sahib, if you know how to
handle the tube. The sahib takes it like a Mussulman. Wah! Wah! Where did he learn that?
His own wedding! Ho! Ho! Ho! The sahib
says that there is no wedding in the matter at all?
Now is it likely that the sahib would speak true
talk to me who am only a black man? Small
wonder, then, that he is in haste. Thirty years
have I beaten the gong at this ford, but never have
I seen a sahib in such haste. Thirty years, sahib!
That is a very long time. Thirty years ago this
ford was on the track of the *bunjaras,* and I have
seen two thousand pack-bullocks cross in one
night. Now the rail has come, and the fire-
carriage says "buz-buz-buz," and a hundred lakhs
of maunds slide across that big bridge. It is very
wonderful; but the ford is lonely now that there
are no *bunjaras* to camp under the trees.

Nay, do not trouble to look at the sky without.
It will rain till the dawn. Listen! The bowlders

are talking to-night in the bed of the river. Hear
them! They would be husking your bones, sahib,
had you tried to cross. See, I will shut the door
and no rain can enter. *Wahi! Ahi! Ugh!*
Thirty years on the banks of the ford! An old
man am I and—where is the oil for the lamp?

*   *   *   *   *   *   *

Your pardon, but, because of my years, I sleep
no sounder than a dog; and you moved to the
door. Look then, sahib. Look and listen. A full
half *kos* from bank to bank is the stream now—
you can see it under the stars—and there are ten
feet of water therein. It will not shrink because
of the anger in your eyes, and it will not be quiet
on account of your curses. Which is louder,
sahib—your voice or the voice of the river? Call
to it—perhaps it will be ashamed. Lie down and
sleep afresh, sahib. I know the anger of the
Barhwi when there has fallen rain in the foot-hills.
I swam the flood once, on a night tenfold worse
than this, and by the favor of God I was released
from death when I had come to the very gates.

May I tell the tale? Very good talk. I will
fill the pipe anew.

Thirty years ago it was, when I was a young
man and had but newly come to the ford. I was
strong then, and the *bunjaras* had no doubt when
I said "this ford is clear." I have toiled all night
up to my shoulder-blades in running water amid
a hundred bullocks mad with fear, and have

brought them across losing not a hoof. When all was done I fetched the shivering men, and they gave me for reward the pick of their cattle—the bell-bullock of the drove. So great was the honor in which I was held! But to-day when the rain falls and the river rises I creep into my hut and whimper like a dog. The strength is gone from me. I am an old man and the fire-carriage has made the ford desolate. They were wont to call me the Strong One of the Barhwi.

Behold my face, sahib. It is the face of a monkey. And my arm. It is the arm of an old woman. I swear to you, sahib, that a woman has loved this face and has rested in the hollow of this arm. Twenty years ago, sahib. Believe me, this was true talk—twenty years ago.

Come to the door and look across. Can you see a thin fire very far away down the stream? That is the temple-fire, in the shrine of Hanuman, of the village of Pateera. North, under the big star, is the village itself, but it is hidden by a bend of the river. Is that far to swim, sahib? Would you take off your clothes and adventure? Yet I swam to Pateera—not once but many times; and there are *muggers* in the river too.

Love knows no caste; else why should I, a Mussulman and the son of a Mussulman, have sought a Hindoo woman—a widow of the Hindoos—the sister of the headman of Pateera? But it was even so. They of the headman's household came on a pilgrimage to Muttra when she was but newly a bride. Silver tires were upon the wheels of the bullock-cart, and silken curtains hid the woman. Sahib, I made no haste in their conveyance, for the wind parted the curtains and I saw her. When they returned from pilgrimage the boy that was her husband had died, and I saw her again in the bullock-cart. By God, these Hindoos are fools! What was it to me whether she was Hindoo or Jain—scavenger, leper or whole? I would have married her and made her a home by the ford. The seventh of the nine bars says that a man may not marry one of the idolators. Is that truth? Both Shiahs and Sunnis say that a Mussulman may not marry one of the idolators? Is the sahib a priest, then, that he knows so much? I will tell him something that he does not know. There is neither Shiah nor Sunni, forbidden nor idolator, in love; and the nine bars are but nine little fagots that the flame of love utterly burns away. In truth, I would have taken her; but what could I do? The headman would have sent his men to break my head with staves. I am not—I was not—afraid of any five men; but against half a village who can prevail?

Therefore it was my custom, these things having been arranged between us twain, to go by night to the village of Pateera, and there we met among the crops; no man knowing aught of the matter. Behold, now! I was wont to cross here, skirting the jungle to the river bend where the railway bridge is, and thence across the elbow of land to Pateera. The light of the shrine was my guide when the nights were dark. That jungle near the river is very full of snakes—little *karaits* that sleep on the sand—and moreover, her brothers would have slain me had they found me in the crops. But none knew—none knew save she and I; and the blown sand of the river bed covered the track of my feet. In the hot months it was an easy thing to pass from the ford to Pateera, and in the first rains, when the river rose slowly, it was an easy thing also. I set the strength of my body against the strength of the stream, and nightly I eat in my hut here and drank at Pateera yonder. She had said that one Hirnam Singh, a scamp, had sought her, and he was of a village up the river but on the same bank. All Sikhs are dogs, and they have refused in their folly that good gift of God—tobacco. I was ready to destroy Hirnam Singh that ever he had come nigh her; and the more because he had sworn to her that she had a lover, and that he would lie in wait and give the name to the head-man unless she went away with him. What curs are these Sikhs!

After that news I swam always with a little sharp knife in my belt, and evil would it have been for a man had he stayed me. I knew not the face of Hirnam Singh, but I would have killed any who came between me and her.

Upon a night in the beginning of the rains I was minded to go across to Pateera, albeit the river was angry. Now the nature of the Barhwi is this, sahib. In twenty breaths it comes down from the hills, a wall three feet high, and I have seen it, between the lighting of a fire and the cooking of a flapjack, grow from the runnel to a sister of the Jumna.

When I left this bank there was a shoal a half mile down, and I made shift to fetch it and draw breath there ere going forward; for I felt the hands of the river heavy upon my heels. Yet what will a young man not do for Love's sake? There was but little light from the stars, and midway to the shoal a branch of the stinking deodar-tree brushed my mouth as I swam. That was a sign of heavy rain in the foot-hills and beyond, for the deodar is a strong tree, not easily shaken from the hill-sides. I made haste, the river aiding me, but ere I had touched the shoal, the pulse of the stream beat, as it were, within me and around, and, behold, the shoal was gone and I rode high on the crest of a wave that ran from bank to bank. Has the sahib ever been cast into much water that fights and will not let a man use his limbs? To me, my head up on the water, it seemed as though there were naught but water to the world's end, and the river drove me with its drift-wood. A man is a very little thing in the belly of a flood. And this flood, though I knew it not, was the Great Flood about which men talk still. My liver was dissolved and I lay like a log upon my back in the fear of death. There were living things in the water, crying and howling grievously—beasts of the forest and cattle, and once the voice of a man asking for help. But the rain came and lashed the water white, and I heard no more save the roar of the bowlders below and the roar of the rain above. Thus I was whirled down-stream, wrestling for the breath in me. It is very hard to die when one is young. Can the sahib, standing here, see the railway bridge? Look, there are the lights of the mail-train going to Peshawur! The bridge is now twenty feet above the river, but upon that night the water was roaring against the lattice-work and against the lattice came I feet first. But much driftwood was piled there and upon the piers, and I took no great hurt. Only the river pressed me as a strong man presses a weaker. Scarcely could I take hold of the lattice-work and crawl to the upper boom. Sahib, the water was foaming across the rails a foot deep! Judge therefore what manner of flood it must have been. I could not hear. I could not see. I could but lie on the boom and pant for breath.

After awhile the rain ceased and there came out in the sky certain new washed stars, and by their light I saw that there was no end to the black water as far as the eye could travel, and the water had risen upon the rails. There were dead beasts in the driftwood on the piers, and others caught by the neck in the lattice-work, and others not yet drowned who strove to find a foot-

the byre of the herdsman's house. But my love
was already there, weeping upon her knees. She
feared that the flood had swept my hut at the
Barhwi Ford. When I came softly through the
ankle-deep water, she thought it was a ghost and
would have fled, but I put my arms around her,
and . . . I was no ghost in those days,
though I am an old man now. Ho! Ho! Dried
corn, in truth. Maize without juice. Ho! Ho!*

I told her the story of the breaking of the
Barhwi Bridge, and she said that I was greater
than mortal man, for none may cross the Barhwi
in full flood, and I had seen what never man had
seen before. Hand in hand we went to the knoll
where the dead lay, and I showed her by what help
I had made the ford. She looked also upon the
body under the stars, for the latter end of the
night was clear, and hid her face in her hands,
crying: "It is the body of Hirnam Singh!" I
said: "The swine is of more use dead than living,
my beloved," and she said: "Surely, for he has
saved the dearest life in the world to my love.
None the less, he cannot stay here, for that would
bring shame upon me." The body was not a
gunshot from her door.

Then said I, rolling the body with my hands:
"God hath judged between us, Hirnam Singh,
that thy blood might not be upon my head. Now,

*I grieve to say that the Warden of the Barhwi Ford is
responsible here for two very bad puns in the vernacular.
—R. K.

whether I have done thee a wrong in keeping thee
from the burning-ghat, do thou and the crows
settle together." So I cast him adrift into the
flood-water, and he was drawn out to the open,
ever wagging his thick black beard like a priest
under the pulpit-board. And I saw no more of
Hirnam Singh.

Before the breaking of the day we two parted,
and I moved toward such of the jungle as was
not flooded. With the full light I saw what I had
done in the darkness, and the bones of my body
were loosened in my flesh, for there ran two *kos*
of raging water between the village of Pateera
and the trees of the far bank, and, in the middle,
the piers of the Barhwi Bridge showed like
broken teeth in the jaw of an old man. Nor was
there any life upon the waters—neither birds nor
boats, but only an army of drowned things—bullocks and horses and men—and the river was red-
der than blood from the clay of the foot-hills.
Never had I seen such a flood—never since that
year have I seen the like—and, oh, sahib, no man
living had done what I had done. There was no
return for me that day. Not for all the lands of
the headman would I venture a second time without the shield of darkness that cloaks danger. I
went a *kos* up the river to the house of a blacksmith, saying that the flood had swept me from
my hut, and they gave me food. Seven days I
stayed with the blacksmith, till a boat came and I
returned to my house. There was no trace of

wall, or roof, or floor—naught but a patch of slimy mud. Judge, therefore, sahib, how far the river must have risen. It was written that I should not die either in my house, or in the heart of the Barhwi, or under the wreck of the Barhwi Bridge, for God sent down Hirnam Singh two days dead, though I know not how the man died, to be my buoy and support. Hirnam Singh has been in hell these twenty years, and the thought of that night must be the flower of his torment.

Listen, sahib! The river has changed its voice. It is going to sleep before the dawn, to which there is yet one hour. With the light it will come down afresh. How do I know? Have I been here thirty years without knowing the voice of the river as a father knows the voice of his son? Every moment it is talking less angrily. I swear that there will be no danger for one hour or, perhaps, two. I can not answer for the morning. Be quick, sahib! I will call Ram Pershad, and he will not turn back this time. Is the 'paulin tightly corded upon all the baggage? *Ohe, mahout* with a mud head, the elephant for the sahib, and tell them on the far side that there will be no crossing after daylight.

Money? Nay, sahib. I am not of that kind. No not even to give sweetmeats to the baby-folk. My house, look you, is empty, and I am an old man.

Dutt, Ram Pershad! *Dutt! Dutt! Dutt!* Good luck go with you, sahib.

THE SENDING OF DANA DA

WHEN the Devil rides on your chest remember the *chamar*.
Native Proverb.

ONCE upon a time, some people in India made a
new heaven and a new earth out of broken tea-
cups, a missing brooch or two, and a hair-brush.
These were hidden under bushes, or stuffed into
holes in the hill-side, and an entire civil service of
subordinate gods used to find or mend them
again; and every one said: "There are more
things in heaven and earth than are dreamed of
in our philosophy." Several other things happened also, but the religion never seemed to get
much beyond its first manifestations; though it
added an air-line postal *dak,* and orchestral effects
in order to keep abreast of the times, and stall
off competition.

This religion was too elastic for ordinary use.
It stretched itself and embraced pieces of everything that medicine-men of all ages have manufactured. It approved of and stole from Free-
masonry; looted the Latter-day Rosicrucians of
half their pet words; took any fragments of
Egyptian philosophy that it found in the En-
cyclopædia Britannica; annexed as many of the
Vedas as had been translated into French or Eng-

lish, and talked of all the rest; built in the German versions of what is left of the Zend Avesta; encouraged white, gray and black magic, including Spiritualism, palmistry, fortune-telling by cards, hot chestnuts, double-kerneled nuts and tallow droppings; would have adopted Voodoo and Oboe had it known anything about them, and showed itself, in every way, one of the most accommodating arrangements that had ever been invented since the birth of the sea.

When it was in thorough working order, with all the machinery down to the subscriptions complete, Dana Da came from nowhere, with nothing in his hands, and wrote a chapter in its history which has hitherto been unpublished. He said that his first name was Dana, and his second was Da. Now, setting aside Dana of the New York "Sun," Dana is a Bhil name, and Da fits no native of India unless you accept the Bengali Dé as the original spelling. Da is Lap or Finnish; and Dana Da was neither Finn, Chin, Bhil, Bengali, Lap, Nair, Gond, Romaney, Magh, Bokhariot, Kurd, Armenian, Levantine, Jew, Persian, Punjabi, Madrasi, Parsee, nor anything else known to ethnologists. He was simply Dana Da, and declined to give further information. For the sake of brevity, and as roughly indicating his origin, he was called "The Native." He might have been the original Old Man of the Mountains, who is said to be the only authorized head of the Tea-cup Creed. Some people said that he was; but Dana Da used to smile and deny any connection with the cult; explaining that he was an "independent experimenter."

As I have said, he came from nowhere, with his hands behind his back, and studied the creed for three weeks; sitting at the feet of those best competent to explain its mysteries. Then he laughed aloud and went away, but the laugh might have been either of devotion or derision.

When he returned he was without money, but his pride was unabated. He declared that he knew more about the things in heaven and earth than those who taught him, and for this contumacy was abandoned altogether.

His next appearance in public life was at a big cantonment in Upper India, and he was then telling fortunes with the help of three leaden dice, a very dirty old cloth, and a little tin box of opium pills. He told better fortunes when he was allowed half a bottle of whisky; but the things which he invented on the opium were quite worth the money. He was in reduced circumstances. Among other people's he told the fortune of an Englishman who had once been interested in the Simla creed, but who, later on, had married and forgotten all his old knowledge in the study of babies and Exchange. The Englishman allowed Dana Da to tell a fortune for charity's sake, and gave him five rupees, a dinner, and some old clothes. When he had eaten, Dana Da professed gratitude, and asked if there were anything he could do for his host—in the esoteric line.

"Is there any one that you love?" said Dana Da. The Englishman loved his wife, but had no desire to drag her name into the conversation. He therefore shook his head.

"Is there any one that you hate?" said Dana Da. The Englishman said that there were several men whom he hated deeply.

"Very good," said Dana Da, upon whom the whisky and the opium were beginning to tell. "Only give me their names, and I will dispatch a Sending to them and kill them."

Now a Sending is a horrible arrangement, first invented, they say, in Iceland. It is a thing sent by a wizard, and may take any form, but, most generally wanders about the land in the shape of a little purple cloud till it finds the sendee, and him it kills by changing into the form of a horse, or a cat, or a man without a face. It is not strictly a native patent, though *chamars* can, if irritated, dispatch a Sending which sits on the breast of their enemy by night and nearly kills him. Very few natives care to irritate *chamars* for this reason.

"Let me dispatch a Sending," said Dana Da; "I am nearly dead now with want, and drink, and opium; but I should like to kill a man before I die. I can send a Sending anywhere you choose, and in any form except in the shape of a man."

The Englishman had no friends that he wished

to kill, but partly to soothe Dana Da, whose eyes were rolling, and partly to see what would be done, he asked whether a modified Sending could not be arranged for—such a Sending as should make a man's life a burden to him, and yet do him no harm. If this were possible, he notified his willingness to give Dana Da ten rupees for the job.

"I am not what I was once," said Dana Da, "and I must take the money because I am poor. To what Englishman shall I send it?"

"Send a Sending to Lone Sahib," said the Englishman, naming a man who had been most bitter in rebuking him for his apostasy from the Teacup Creed. Dana Da laughed and nodded.

"I could have chosen no better man myself," said he. "I will see that he finds the Sending about his path and about his bed."

He lay down on the hearth-rug, turned up the whites of his eyes, shivered all over and began to snort. This was magic, or opium, or the Sending, or all three. When he opened his eyes he vowed that the Sending had started upon the warpath, and was at that moment flying up to the town where Lone Sahib lives.

"Give me my ten rupees," said Dana Da, wearily, "and write a letter to Lone Sahib, telling him, and all who believe with him, that you and a friend are using a power greater than theirs. They will see that you are speaking the truth."

kind. Their letters dropped from the ceiling—unstamped—and spirits used to squatter up and down their staircases all night. But they had never come into contact with kittens. Lone Sahib wrote out the facts, noting the hour and the minute, as every psychical observer is bound to do, and appending the Englishman's letter because it was the most mysterious document and might have had a bearing upon anything in this world or the next. An outsider would have translated all the tangle thus: "Look out! You laughed at me once, and now I am going to make you sit up."

Lone Sahib's coreligionists found that meaning in it; but their translation was refined and full of four-syllable words. They held a sederunt, and were filled with tremulous joy, for, in spite of their familiarity with all the other worlds and cycles, they had a very human awe of things sent from ghost-land. They met in Lone Sahib's room in shrouded and sepulchral gloom, and their conclave was broken up by the clinking among the photo-frames on the mantel-piece. A wee white kitten, nearly blind, was looping and writhing itself between the clock and the candle-sticks. That stopped all investigations or doubtings. Here was the manifestation in the flesh. It was, so far as could be seen, devoid of purpose, but it was a manifestation of undoubted authenticity.

They drafted a round robin to the Englishman, the backslider of old days, adjuring him in

the interests of the creed to explain whether there
was any connection between the embodiment of
some Egyptian god or other (I have forgotten
the name) and his communication. They called
the kitten Ra, or Toth, or Shem, or Noah, or
something; and when Lone Sahib confessed that
the first one had, at his most misguided instance,
been drowned by the sweeper, they said consol-
ingly that in his next life he would be a
"bounder," and not even a "rounder" of the low-
est grade. These words may not be quite correct, but they express the sense of the house ac-
curately.

When the Englishman received the round robin
—it came by post—he was startled and bewildered. He sent into the bazaar for Dana Da,
who read the letter and laughed. "That is my
Sending," said he. "I told you I would work
well. Now give me another ten rupees."

"But what in the world is this gibberish about
Egyptian gods?" asked the Englishman.

"Cats," said Dana Da, with a hiccough, for
he had discovered the Englishman's whisky
bottle. "Cats and cats and cats! Never was
such a Sending. A hundred of cats. Now give
me ten more rupees and write as I dictate."

Dana Da's letter was a curiosity. It bore the
Englishman's signature, and hinted at cats—a
Sending of cats. The mere words on paper were
creepy and uncanny to behold.

"What have you done, though?" said the Eng-

lishman; "I am as much in the dark as ever. Do
you mean to say that you can actually send this
absurd Sending you talk about?"

"Judge for yourself," said Dana Da. "What
does that letter mean? In a little time they will
be all at my feet and yours, and I, oh, glory! will
be drugged or drunk all day long."

Dana Da knew his people.

When a man who hates cats wakes up in the
morning and finds a little squirming kitten on his
breast, or puts his hand into his ulster-pocket and
finds a little half-dead kitten where his gloves
should be, or opens his trunk and finds a vile kitten among his dress-shirts, or goes for a long
ride with his mackintosh strapped on his saddle-
bow and shakes a little squawling kitten from its
folds when he opens it, or goes out to dinner and
finds a little blind kitten under his chair, or stays
at home and finds a writhing kitten under the
quilt, or wriggling among his boots, or hanging,
head downward, in his tobacco-jar, or being
mangled by his terrier in the veranda—when
such a man finds one kitten, neither more nor
less, once a day in a place where no kitten rightly
could or should be, he is naturally upset. When
he dare not murder his daily trove because he believes it to be a manifestation, an emissary, an
embodiment, and half a dozen other things all out
of the regular course of nature, he is more than
upset. He is actually distressed. Some of Lone
Sahib's coreligionists thought that he was a

highly favored individual; but many said that if
he had treated the first kitten with proper respect
—as suited a Toth-Ra-Tum-Sennacherib Embodiment—all this trouble would have been
averted. They compared him to the Ancient
Mariner, but none the less they were proud of
him and proud of the Englishman who had sent
the manifestation. They did not call it a Sending because Icelandic magic was not in their program.

After sixteen kittens—that is to say, after
one fortnight, for there were three kittens on the
first day to impress the fact of the Sending, the
whole camp was uplifted by a letter—it came flying through a window—from the Old Man of the
Mountains—the head of all the creed—explaining
the manifestation in the most beautiful language
and soaking up all the credit of it for himself.
The Englishman, said the letter, was not there at
all. He was a backslider without power or as-
ceticism, who couldn't even raise a table by force
of volition, much less project an army of kittens
through space. The entire arrangement, said the
letter, was strictly orthodox, worked and sanc-
tioned by the highest authorities within the pale
of the creed. There was great joy at this, for
some of the weaker brethren seeing that an outsider who had been working on independent lines
could create kittens, whereas their own rules had
never gone beyond crockery—and broken at that
—were showing a desire to break line on their

own trail. In fact, there was the promise of a schism. A second round robin was drafted to the Englishman, beginning: "Oh, Scoffer," and ending with a selection of curses from the rites of Mizraim and Memphis and the Commination of Jugana who was a "fifth-rounder," upon whose name an upstart "third-rounder" once traded. A papal excommunication is a *billet-doux* compared to the Commination of Jugana. The Englishman had been proved under the hand and seal of the Old Man of the Mountains to have appropriated virtue and pretended to have power which, in reality, belonged only to the supreme head. Naturally the round robin did not spare him.

He handed the letter to Dana Da to translate into decent English. The effect on Dana Da was curious. At first he was furiously angry, and then he laughed for five minutes.

"I had thought," he said, "that they would have come to me. In another week I would have shown that I sent the Sending, and they would have discrowned the Old Man of the Mountains who has sent this Sending of mine. Do you do nothing? The time has come for me to act. Write as I dictate, and I will put them to shame. But give me ten more rupees."

At Dana Da's dictation the Englishman wrote nothing less than a formal challenge to the Old Man of the Mountains. It wound up: "And if this manifestation be from your hand, then let it

go forward; but it if be from my hand, I will
that the Sending shall cease in two days' time.
On that day there shall be twelve kittens and
thenceforward none at all. The people shall
judge between us." This was signed by Dana
Da, who added pentacles and pentagrams, and a
crux ansata, and half a dozen *swastikas,* and a
Triple Tau to his name, just to show that he was
all he laid claim to be.

The challenge was read out to the gentlemen
and ladies, and they remembered then that Dana
Da had laughed at them some years ago. It was
officially announced that the Old Man of the
Mountains would treat the matter with contempt;
Dana Da being an independent investigator without a single "round" at the back of him. But this
did not soothe his people. They wanted to see a
fight. They were very human for all their spirituality. Lone Sahib, who was really being worn
out with kittens, submitted meekly to his fate. He
felt that he was being "kittened to prove the
power of Dana Da," as the poet says.

When the stated day dawned, the shower of
kittens began. Some were white and some were
tabby, and all were about the same loathsome age.
Three were on his hearth-rug, three in his bath-
room, and the other six turned up at intervals
among the visitors who came to see the prophecy
break down. Never was a more satisfactory
Sending. On the next day there were no kittens, and the next day and all the other days were

kittenless and quiet. The people murmured and looked to the Old Man of the Mountains for an explanation. A letter, written on a palm-leaf, dropped from the ceiling, but every one except Lone Sahib felt that letters were not what the occasion demanded. There should have been cats, there should have been cats—full-grown ones. The letter proved conclusively that there had been a hitch in the psychic current which, colliding with a dual identity, had interfered with the percipient activity all along the main line. The kittens were still going on, but owing to some failure in the developing fluid, they were not materialized. The air was thick with letters for a few days afterward. Unseen hands played Glück and Beethoven in finger-bowls and clock-shades; but all men felt that psychic life was a mockery without materialized kittens. Even Lone Sahib shouted with the majority on this head. Dana Da's letters were very insulting, and if he had then offered to lead a new departure, there is no knowing what might not have happened.

But Dana Da was dying of whisky and opium in the Englishman's godown, and had small heart for new creeds.

"They have been put to shame," said he. "Never was such a Sending. It has killed me."

"Nonsense," said the Englishman, "you are going to die, Dana Da, and that sort of stuff must be left behind. I'll admit that you have made

some queer things come about. Tell me honestly,
now, how was it done?"

"Give me ten more rupees," said Dana Da,
faintly, "and if I die before I spend them, bury
them with me." The silver was counted out
while Dana Da was fighting with death. His
hand closed upon the money and he smiled a grim
smile.

"Bend low," he whispered. The Englishman
bent.

"*Bunnia*—mission-school—expelled—*box-wal-
lah* (peddler)—Ceylon pearl-merchant—all mine
English education—outcasted, and made up name
Dana Da—England with American thought-
reading man and—and—you gave me ten rupees
several times—I gave the Sahib's bearer two-
eight a month for cats—little, little cats. I wrote,
and he put them about—very clever man. Very
few kittens now in the bazaar. Ask Lone Sahib's
sweeper's wife."

So saying, Dana Da gasped and passed away
into a land where, if all be true, there are no
materializations and the making of new creeds is
discouraged.

But consider the gorgeous simplicity of it all!

UNDER THE DEODARS

THE EDUCATION OF OTIS YEERE

I

SHOWING HOW THE GREAT IDEA WAS BORN

> In the pleasant orchard closes
> "God bless all our gains," say we;
> But "May God bless all our losses,"
> Better suits with our degree.
> —*The Lost Bower.*

THIS is the history of a Failure; but the woman who failed said it might be an instructive tale to put into print for the benefit of the younger generation. The younger generation does not want instruction. It is perfectly willing to instruct if any one will listen to it. None the less, here begins the story where every right-minded story should begin, that is to say, at Simla, where all things begin and many come to an evil end.

The mistake was due to a very clever woman making a blunder and not retrieving it. Men are licensed to stumble, but a clever woman's mistake is outside the regular course of Nature and Providence; since all good people know that a woman is the only infallible thing in this world, except Government paper of the '79 issue, bearing interest at four and a half per cent. Yet, we have to remember that six consecutive days of rehearsing the star-part of "The Fallen Angel," at the New Gaiety Theater, where the plaster is not yet properly dry, might have brought about an unhingement of spirits which, again, might have led to eccentricities.

Mrs. Hauksbee came to "The Foundry" to tiffin with Mrs. Mallowe, her one bosom friend, for she was in no sense "a woman's woman." And it was a woman's tiffin, the door shut to all the world; and they both talked chiffons, which is French for Mysteries.

"I've enjoyed an interval of sanity," Mrs. Hauksbee announced, after tiffin was over and the two were comfortably settled in the little writing-room that opened out of Mrs. Mallowe's bedroom.

"My dear girl, what has *he* done?" said Mrs. Mallowe, sweetly. It is noticeable that ladies of a certain age call each other "dear girl," just as commissioners of twenty-eight years' standing address their equals in the Civil List as "my boy."

"There's no *he* in the case. Who am I that an imaginary man should be always credited to me? Am I an Apache?"

"No, dear; but somebody's scalp is generally drying at your wigwam door. Soaking, rather."

This was an illusion to the Hawley Boy, who was in the habit of riding all across Simla in the Rains, to call on Mrs. Hauksbee. That lady laughed. "For my sins, the Aide at Tryconnel last night told me off to The Mussuck. Hush! Don't laugh. One of my most devoted admirers. When duff came in—some one really ought to teach them to make puddings at Tryconnel—The Mussuck was at liberty to attend me."

"Sweet soul! I know his appetite," said Mrs. Mallowe. "Did he, oh, *did* he, begin his wooing?"

"By a special mercy of Providence, *no*. He explained his importance as a Pillar of the Empire. I didn't laugh."

"Lucy, I don't believe you."

"Ask Captain Sangar; he was on the other side. Well, as I was saying, The Mussuck dilated."

"I think I can see him doing it," said Mrs. Mallowe, pensively, scratching her fox-terrier's ears.

"I was properly impressed. Most properly. I yawned openly. 'Strict supervision, and play them off one against the other,' said The Mussuck, shoveling down his ice by tureenfuls, I assure you. *'That,* Mrs. Hauksbee, is the secret of our Government.'"

Mrs. Mallowe laughed long and merrily. "And what did *you* say?"

"Did you ever know me at loss for an answer yet? I said: 'So I have observed in my dealings with you.' The Mussuck swelled with pride. He is coming to call on me to-morrow. The Hawley Boy is coming too."

"'Strict supervision, and play them off one against the other. *That,* Mrs. Hauksbee, is the secret of *our* Government.' And I dare say if we could get to The Mussuck's heart, we should find that he considers himself a man of the world."

"As he is on the other two things. I like The Mussuck, and I won't have you call him names. He amuses me."

"He has reformed you, too, by what appears. Explain the interval of sanity, and hit Tim on the nose with the paper-cutter, please. That dog is too fond of sugar. Do you take milk in yours?"

"No, thanks. Polly, I'm wearied of this life. It's hollow."

"Turn religious, then. I always said that Rome would be your fate."

"Only exchanging half a dozen *attachés* in red for one in black, and if I fasted, the wrinkles would come, and never, *never* go. Has it struck you, dear, that I'm getting old?"

"Thanks for your courtesy. I'll return it. Ye-es, we are both not exactly—how shall I put it?"

"What we have been. 'I feel it in my bones,' as Mrs. Crossley says. Polly, I've wasted my life."

"As how?"

"Never mind how. I feel it. I want to be a Power before I die."

"*Be* a Power then. You've wits enough for anything . . . and beauty?"

Mrs. Hauksbee pointed a tea-spoon straight at her hostess. "Polly, if you heap compliments on me like this, I shall cease to believe that you're a woman. Tell me how I am to be a Power."

"Inform The Mussuck that he is the most fascinating and slimmest man in Asia, and he'll tell
you anything and everything you please."

"Bother The Mussuck! I mean an *intellectual*
Power—not a *gas*-power. Polly, I'm going to
start a salon."

Mrs. Mallowe turned lazily on the sofa and
rested her head on her hand. "Hear the words of
the Preacher, the son of Baruch."

"*Will* you talk sensibly?"

"I will, dear, for I see that you are going to
make a mistake."

"I never made a mistake in my life—at least,
never one that I couldn't explain away afterward."

"Going to make a mistake," went on Mrs. Mallowe, composedly. "It is impossible to start a
salon in Simla. A *bar* would be much more to
the point."

"Perhaps; but why? It seems so easy."

"Just what makes it so difficult. How many
clever women are there in Simla?"

"Myself and yourself," said Mrs. Hauksbee,
without a moment's hesitation.

"Modest woman! Mrs. Feardon would thank
you for that. And how many clever men?"

"Oh—er—hundreds," said Mrs. Hauksbee,
vaguely.

"What a fatal blunder! Not *one*. They are
all bespoke by the Government. Take my husband, for instance. Jack *was* a clever man, though
I say so who shouldn't. Government has eaten

him up. All his ideas and powers of conversation
—he really used to be a good talker, even to his
wife, in the old days—are taken from him by this
—this kitchen-sink of a Government. That's the
case with every man up here who is at work. I
don't suppose a Russian convict under the knout
is able to amuse the rest of his gang; and all our
men-folk here are gilded convicts."

"But there are scores—"

"I know what you're going to say. Scores of
idle men up on leave. I admit it, but they are all
of two objectionable sets. The Civilian who'd be
delightful if he had the military man's knowledge
of the world and style, and the military man
who'd be adorable if he had the Civilian's cul-
ture."

"Detestable word! *Have* Civilians Culchaw?
I never studied the breed deeply."

"Don't make fun of Jack's service. Yes.
They're like the teapoys in the Lakka Bazar—
good material, but not polished. They can't help
themselves, poor dears. A Civilian only *begins*
to be tolerable after he has knocked about the
world for fifteen years."

"And a military man?"

"When he has had the same amount of service.
The young of both species are *horrible*. You
would have scores of them in your salon."

"I would *not*!" said Mrs. Hauksbee, fiercely.
"I would tell the bearer to darwaza band them.
I'd put their own colonels and commissioners at

the door to turn them away. I'd give them to the Topsham girl to play with."

"The Topsham girl would be grateful for the gift. But to go back to the salon. Allowing that you had gathered all your men and women together, what would you do with them? Make them talk? They would all with one accord begin to flirt. Your salon would become a glorified Peliti's—a 'Scandal Point' by lamplight."

"There's a certain amount of wisdom in that view."

"There's all the wisdom in the world in it. Surely, twelve Simla seasons ought to have taught you that you can't focus *anything* in India; and a salon, to be any good at all, *must* be permanent. In two seasons your roomful would be scattered all over Asia. We are only little bits of dirt on the hill-sides—here one day and blown down the khud the next. We have lost the art of talking—at least our men have. We have no cohesion—"

"George Eliot in the flesh," interpolated Mrs. Hauksbee, wickedly.

"And collectively, my dear scoffer, we, men and women alike, have *no* influence. Come into the veranda and look at the Mall."

The two looked down on the now rapidly filling road, for all Simla was abroad to steal a stroll between a shower and a fog.

"How do you propose to fix that river? Look! There's the Mussuck—head of goodness knows what. He is a power in the land, though he *does* eat like a coster-monger. There's Colonel Blone, and General Grucher, and Sir Dugald Delane, and Sir Henry Haughton, and Mr. Jellalatty. All Heads of Departments, and all powerful."

"And all my fervent admirers," said Mrs. Hauksbee, piously. "Sir Henry Haughton raves about me. But go on."

"One by one, these men are worth something. Collectively, they're just a mob of Anglo-Indians. Who cares for what Anglo-Indians say? Your salon won't weld the Departments together and make you mistress of India, dear. And these creatures won't talk administrative 'shop' in a crowd—your salon—because they are so afraid of the men in the lower ranks overhearing it. They have forgotten what of Literature and Art they ever knew, and the women—"

"Can't talk about anything except the last Gymkhana, or the sins of their last dhai. I was calling on Mrs. Derwills this morning."

"You admit that? They can talk to the subalterns though, and the subalterns can talk to them. Your salon would suit their views admirably, if you respected the religious prejudices of the country and provided plenty of kala juggahs."

"Plenty of kala juggahs. Oh, my poor little idea! Kala juggahs in a salon! But who made *you* so awfully clever?"

"Perhaps I've tried myself; or perhaps I know a woman who has. I have preached and expounded the whole matter, and the conclusion thereof—"

"You needn't go on. 'Is Vanity.' Polly, I thank you. These vermin"—Mrs. Hauksbee waved her hand from the veranda to two men in the crowd below who had raised their hats to her—"these vermin shall not rejoice in a new Scandal Point or an extra Peliti's. I will abandon the notion of a salon. It *did* seem so tempting, though. But what shall I do? I must do something."

"Why? Are not Abana and Pharphar—"

"Jack has made you nearly as bad as himself! I want to, of course. I'm tired of everything and everybody, from a moonlight picnic at Seepee, to the blandishments of The Mussuck."

"Yes—that comes, too, sooner or later. Have you nerve enough to make your bow yet?"

Mrs. Hauksbee's mouth shut grimly. Then she laughed. "I think I see myself doing it. Big Pink placards on the Mall: 'Mrs. Hauksbee! Positively her last appearance on *any* stage! This is to give notice!' No more dances; no more rides or luncheons; no more theatricals with supper to follow; no more sparring with one's dearest, dearest friend; no more fencing with an inconvenient man who hasn't wit enough to clothe what he's pleased to call his sentiments in passable speech; no more parading of The Mussuck while Mrs. Tarkass calls all round Simla, spreading horrible stories about me! No more of anything

that is thoroughly wearying, abominable and detestable, but, all the same, makes life worth the
having. Yes! I see it all! Don't interrupt,
Polly, I'm inspired. A mauve and white striped
'cloud' round my venerable shoulders, a seat in the
fifth row of the Gaiety, and *both* horses sold. Delightful vision! A comfortable arm-chair situ-
ated in three different draughts at every ball-
room; and nice, large, sensible shoes for all the
couples to stumble over as they go into the veranda! Then at supper. Can't you imagine the
scene? The greedy mob gone away. Reluctant
subaltern, pink all over like a newly powdered
baby—they really ought to *tan* subalterns before
they are exported—Polly—sent back by the hostess to do his duty. Slouches up to me across the
room, tugging at a glove two sizes too large for
him—I *hate* a man who wears gloves like over-
coats—and trying to look as if he'd thought of it
from the first. 'May I ah-have the pleasure 'f
takin' you 'nt' supper?' Then I get up with a
hungry smile. Just like this."

"Lucy, how *can* you be so absurd?"

"And sweep out on his arm. So! After supper I shall go away early, you know, because I
shall be afraid of catching cold. No one will look
for my 'rickshaw. *Mine,* so please you! I shall
stand, always with that mauve and white 'cloud'
over my head, while the wet soaks into my dear,
old, venerable feet and Tom swears and shouts
for the memsahib's gharri. Then home to bed at

half past eleven! Truly excellent life—helped out by the visits of the Padri, just fresh from burying somebody down below there." She pointed through the pines, toward the cemetery, and continued with vigorous dramatic gesture:

"Listen! I see it all—down, down even to the stays! *Such* stays! Six-eight a pair, Polly, with red flannel—or list, is it?—that they put into the top of those fearful things. I can draw you a picture of them."

"Lucy, for Heaven's sake, don't go waving your arms about in that idiotic manner! Recollect, every one can see you from the Mall."

"Let them see! They'll think I am rehearsing for 'The Fallen Angel.' Look! There's The Mussuck. How badly he rides. There!"

She blew a kiss to the venerable Indian administrator with infinite grace.

"Now," she continued, "he'll be chaffed about that at the Club in the delicate manner those brutes of men affect, and the Hawley Boy will tell me all about it—softening the details for fear of shocking me. That boy is too good to live, Polly. I've serious thoughts of recommending him to throw up his commission and go into the Church. In his present frame of mind he would obey me. Happy, happy child!"

"Never again," said Mrs. Mallowe, with an affectation of indignation, "shall you tiffin here! 'Lucindy, your behavior is scand'lus.'"

"All your fault," returned Mrs. Hauksbee, "for

suggesting such a thing as my abdication. No! *Jamais*—Nevaire! I will act, dance, ride, frivol, talk scandal, dine out, and appropriate the legitimate captives of any woman I choose, until I d-r-r-rop, or a better woman than I puts me to shame before all Simla . . . and it's dust and ashes in my mouth while I'm doing it!"

She dashed into the drawing-room. Mrs. Mallowe followed and put an arm round her waist.

"I'm *not*!" said Mrs. Hauksbee, defiantly, rummaging in the bosom of her dress for her handkerchief. "I've been dining out for the last ten nights, and rehearsing in the afternoon. You'd be tired yourself. It's only because I'm tired."

Mrs. Mallowe did not at once overwhelm Mrs. Hauksbee with spoken pity or ask her to lie down. She knew her friend too well. Handing her another cup of tea, she went on with the conversation.

"I've been through that too, dear," she said.

"I remember," said Mrs. Hauksbee, a gleam of fun on her face. "In '84, wasn't it? You went out a great deal less next season."

Mrs. Mallowe smiled in a superior and sphinx-like fashion.

"I became an Influence," said she.

"Good gracious, child, you didn't join the Theosophists and kiss Buddha's big toe, did you? I tried to get into their set once, but they cast me out for a skeptic—without a chance of improving my poor little mind, too."

"No, I didn't Theosophilander. Jack says——"

"Never mind Jack. What a husband says is not of the least importance. What did you do?"

"I made a lasting impression."

"So have I—for four months. But that didn't console me in the least. I hated the man. Will you stop smiling in that inscrutable way and tell me what you mean?"

Mrs. Mallowe told.

✱   *   *   *   *   *   *

"And—you—mean—to—say that it is absolutely Platonic on both sides?"

"Absolutely, or I should never have taken it up."

"And his last promotion was due to you?"

Mrs. Mallowe nodded.

"And you warned him against the Topsham girl?"

Another nod.

"And told him of Sir Dugald Delane's private Memo. about him?"

A third nod.

"Why?"

"What a question to ask a woman! Because it amused me at first. I am proud of my property now. If I live, he shall continue to be successful. Yes, I will put him upon the straight road to Knighthood, and everything else that a man values. The rest depends upon himself."

"Polly, you are a most extraordinary woman."

"Not in the least.   I'm concentrated, that's all.
You diffuse yourself, dear; and though all Simla
knows your skill in managing a Team—"

"Can't you choose a prettier word?"

"*Team,* of half a dozen, from The Mussuck to
the Hawley Boy, you gain nothing by it.   Not
even amusement."

"And you?"

"Try my recipe.   Take a man, not a boy, mind,
but an almost mature, unattached man, and be his
guide, philosopher, and friend.   You'll find it *the*
most interesting occupation that you ever em-
barked on.   It can be done—you needn't look
like that—because I've done it."

"There's an element of danger about it that
makes the notion attractive.   I'll get such a man
and say to him: 'Now there must be no flirtation.   Do exactly what I tell you, profit by my
instruction and counsels, and all will yet be well,'
as Toole says.   Is that the idea?"

"More or less," said Mrs. Mallowe, with an
unfathomable smile.   "But be sure he understands
that there must be no flirtation."

II

SHOWING WHAT WAS BORN OF THE GREAT IDEA.

> Dribble-dribble—trickle-trickle—
> What a lot of raw dust!
> My dollie's had an accident
> And out came all the sawdust!
> —*Nursery Rhyme.*

So Mrs. Hauksbee, in "The Foundry" which overlooks Simla Mall, sat at the feet of Mrs. Mallowe and gathered wisdom. The end of the Conference was the Great Idea upon which Mrs. Hauksbee so plumed herself.

"I warn you," said Mrs. Mallowe, beginning to repent of her suggestion, "that the matter is not half so easy as it looks. Any woman—even the Topsham girl—can catch a man, but very, *very* few know how to manage him when captured."

"My child," was the answer, "I've been a female St. Simon Stylites looking down upon men for these—these years past. Ask The Mussuck whether I can manage them."

Mrs. Hauksbee departed humming: "I'll go to him and say to him in manner most ironical." Mrs. Mallowe laughed to herself. Then she grew suddenly sober. "I wonder whether I've done well in advising that amusement? Lucy's a clever woman, but a *thought* too mischievous where a man is concerned."

A week later, the two met at a Monday Pop. "Well?" said Mrs. Mallowe.

"I've caught him!" said Mrs. Hauksbee. Her eyes were dancing with merriment.

"Who is it, you mad woman? I'm sorry I ever spoke to you about it."

"Look between the pillars. In the third row; fourth from the end. You can see his face now. Look!"

"Otis Yeere! Of *all* the improbable people! I don't believe you."

"Hush! Wait till Mrs. Tarkass begins murdering Milton Wellings, and I'll tell you all about it. *S-s-ss!* There we are. That woman's voice always reminds me of an Underground train coming into Earl's Court with the brakes down. Now listen. It is *really* Otis Yeere."

"So I see, but it doesn't follow that he is your property."

"He *is!* By right of trove, as the barristers say. I found him, lonely and unbefriended, the very next night after our talk, at the Dugald Delane's burra-khana. I liked his eyes, and I talked to him. Next day he called. Next day we went for a ride together, and to-day he's tied to my 'rickshaw-wheels hand and foot. You'll see when the concert's over. He doesn't know I'm here yet."

"Thank goodness you haven't chosen a boy.

What are you going to do with him, assuming that you've got him?"

"Assuming, indeed! Does a woman—do *I*—ever make a mistake in that sort of thing? First" —Mrs. Hauksbee ticked off the items ostentatiously on her daintily gloved fingers—"First, my dear, I shall *dress* him properly. At present his raiment is a disgrace, and he wears a dress-shirt like a crumpled sheet of the 'Pioneer.' Secondly, after I have made him presentable, I shall form his *manners*—his morals are above reproach."

"You seem to have discovered a great deal about him considering the shortness of your acquaintance."

"Surely *you* ought to know that the first proof a man gives of his interest in a woman is by talking to her about his own sweet self. If the woman listens without yawning, he begins to like her. If she flatters the animal's vanity, he ends by adoring her."

"In some cases."

"Never mind the exceptions. I know which one you are thinking of. Thirdly, and lastly, after he is polished and made pretty, I shall, as you said, be his guide, philosopher, and friend, and he shall become a success—as great a success as your friend. I always wondered how that man got on. *Did* The Mussuck come to you with the Civil List, and, dropping on one knee—no, two knees, *à la Gibbon*—hand it to you and say: 'Adorable angel, choose your friend's appointment?' "

"Lucy, your long experiences of the Military Department have demoralized you. One doesn't do that sort of thing on the Civil Side."

"No disrespect meant to 'Jack's Service,' my dear. I only asked for information. Give me three months, and see what changes I shall work in my prey."

"Go your own way since you must. But I'm sorry that I was weak enough to suggest the amusement."

" 'I am all discretion, and may be trusted to an in-finite extent,' " quoted Mrs. Hauksbee from "The Fallen Angel;" and the conversation ceased with Mrs. Tarkass's last long-drawn war-whoop.

Her bitterest enemies—and she had many—could hardly accuse Mrs. Hauksbee of wasting her time. Otis Yeere was one of those wandering "dumb" characters, foredoomed through life to be "nobody's property." Ten years in Her Majesty's Bengal Civil Service, spent, for the most part, in undesirable Districts, had dowered him with little to be proud of, and nothing to give confidence. Old enough to have lost the "first fine careless rapture" that showers on the immature 'Stunt imaginary Commissionerships and Stars, and sends him into the cellar with coltish earnestness and abandon; too young to be yet able to look back upon the progress he had made, and thank Providence that under the conditions of to-day he had come even so far, he stood upon the "dead-center" of his career. And when a man stands still, he feels the slightest impulse from without. Fortune had ruled that Otis Yeere should be, for the first part of his service, one of the rank and file who are ground up in the wheels of the Administration, losing heart and soul, and mind and strength, in the process. Until steam replaces manual power in the working of the Empire, there must always be this percentage—must always be the men who are used up, expended, in the mere mechanical routine. For these promotion is far off, and the mill-grind of every day very near and instant. The Secretariats know them only by name; they are not the picked men of the Districts with the Divisions and Collectorates awaiting them. They are simply the rank and file —the food for fever—sharing with the ryot and the plow-bullock the honor of being the plinth on which the State rests. The older ones have lost their aspirations; the younger are putting theirs aside with a sigh. Both learn to endure patiently until the end of the day. Twelve years in the rank and file, men say, will sap the hearts of the bravest and dull the wits of the most keen.

Out of this life Otis Yeere had fled for a few months, drifting, for the sake of a little masculine society, into Simla. When his leave was over he would return to his swampy, sour-green, under-manned district, the native Assistant, the native Doctor, the native Magistrate, the steaming, sweltering Station, the ill-kempt City, and the undisguised insolence of the Municipality that babbled

away the lives of men. Life was cheap, however.
The soil spawned humanity, as it bred frogs in
the Rains, and the gap of the sickness of one
season was filled to overflowing by the fecundity
of the next. Otis was unfeignedly thankful to
lay down his work for a little while and escape
from the seething, whining, weakly hive, impotent
to help itself, but strong in its power to cripple,
thwart, and annoy the weary-eyed man who, by
official irony, was said to be "in charge" of it.

*   *   *   *   *   *   *

"I knew there were women-dowdies in Bengal.
They come up here sometimes. But I didn't know
that there were men-dowdies, too."

Then, for the first time, it occurred to Otis
Yeere that his clothes were rather ancestral in
appearance. It will be seen from the above that
his friendship with Mrs. Hauksbee had made
great strides.

As that lady truthfully says, a man is never so
happy as when he is talking about himself. From
Otis Yeere's lips Mrs. Hauksbee, before long,
learned everything that she wished to know about
the subject of her experiment; learned what manner of life he had led in what she vaguely called
"those awful cholera districts;" learned, too, but
this knowledge came later, what manner of life
he had purposed to lead, and what dreams he had
dreamed in the year of grace '77, before the reality

had knocked the heart out of him.   Very pleasant
are the shady bridle-paths round Prospect Hill for
the telling of confidences.

"Not yet," said Mrs. Hauksbee to Mrs. Mallowe.   "Not yet.   I must wait until the man is
properly dressed, at least.   Great heavens, is it
possible that he doesn't know what an honor it is
to be taken up by *Me!*"

Mrs. Hauksbee did not reckon false modesty
as one of her failings.

"Always with Mrs. Hauksbee!" murmured
Mrs. Mallowe, with her sweetest smile, to Otis.
"Oh, you men, you men!   Here are our Punjabis
growling because you've monopolized the nicest
woman in Simla.   They'll tear you to pieces on the
Mall, some day, Mr. Yeere."

Mrs. Mallowe rattled down-hill, having satisfied herself, by a glance through the fringe of her
sunshade, of the effect of her words.

The shot went home.   Of a surety Otis Yeere
was somebody in this bewildering whirl of Simla.
Had monopolized the nicest woman in it, and the
Punjabis were growling.   The notion justified a
mild glow of vanity.   He had never regarded his
acquaintance with Mrs. Hauksbee as a matter for
general interest.

The knowledge of envy was a pleasant feeling
to the man of no account.   It was intensified later
in the day when a luncher at the Club said spite-
fully: "Well, for a debilitated Ditcher, Yeere,
you are going it.   Hasn't any kind friend told

you that she's the most dangerous woman in Simla?"

Yeere chuckled and passed out. When, oh, when, would his new clothes be ready? He descended into the Mall to inquire; and Mrs Hauksbee, coming over the Church Ridge in her 'rickshaw, looked down upon him approvingly. "He's learning to carry himself as if he were a man, instead of a piece of furniture, and"—she screwed up her eyes to see the better through the sunlight—"he *is* a man when he holds himself like that. Oh, blessed Conceit, what should we be without you?"

With the new clothes came a new stock of self-confidence. Otis Yeere discovered that he could enter a room without breaking into a gentle perspiration, and could cross one, even to talk to Mrs. Hauksbee, as though rooms were meant to be crossed. He was, for the first time in nine years, proud of himself, and contented with his life, satisfied with his new clothes, and rejoicing in the coveted friendship of Mrs. Hauksbee.

"Conceit is what the poor fellow wants," she said in confidence to Mrs. Mallowe. "I believe they must use the Civilians to plow the fields with in Lower Bengal. You see, I have to begin from the very beginning—haven't I? But you'll admit, won't you, dear, that he is immensely improved since I took him in hand? Only give me a little more time and he won't know himself."

Indeed, Yeere was rapidly beginning to forget

what he had been. One of his own rank and file put the matter in a nutshell when he asked Yeere, in reference to nothing: "And who has been making *you* a Member of Council, lately? You carry the side of half a dozen of 'em."

"I—I'm awf'ly sorry. I didn't mean it, you know," said Yeere, apologetically.

"There'll be no holding you," continued the old stager, grimly. "Climb down, Otis—climb down, and get all that beastly affectation knocked out of you with fever! Three thousand a month won't support it."

Yeere repeated the incident to Mrs. Hauksbee. He had insensibly come to look upon her as his Frau Confessorin.

"And you apologized!" she said. "Oh, shame! I *hate* a man who apologizes. Never apologize for what your friend called 'side.' *Never!* It's a man's *business* to be insolent and overbearing until he meets with a stronger. Now, you bad boy, listen to me."

Simply and straightforwardly, as the 'rickshaw loitered round Jakko, Mrs. Hauksbee preached to Otis Yeere the Great Gospel of Conceit, illustrating it with living subjects encountered during their Sunday afternoon stroll.

"Good gracious!" she concluded with the personal argument, "you'll apologize next for being my *attaché?*"

"Never!" said Otis Yeere. "That's another thing altogether. I shall always be—"

"What's coming?" thought Mrs. Hauksbee.

"Proud of that," said Otis.

"Safe for the present," she said to herself.

"But I'm afraid I *have* grown conceited. Like Jeshurun, you know. When he waxed fat, then he kicked. It's the having no worry on one's mind and the Hill air, I suppose."

"Hill air, indeed!" said Mrs. Hauksbee to herself. "He'd have been hiding in the Club till the last day of his leave, if I hadn't discovered him." Then aloud:

"Why shouldn't you be? You have every right to."

"I! Why?"

"Oh, hundreds of things. I'm not going to waste this lovely afternoon by explaining; but I *know* you have. What was that heap of manuscript you showed me about the grammar of the aboriginal—what's their names?"

"Gullals. A piece of nonsense. I've far too much work to do to bother over Gullals now. You should see my District. Come down with your husband some day and I'll show you round. Such a lovely place in the Rains! A sheet of water with the railway embankment and the snakes sticking out, and, in the summer, green flies and green squash. The people would die of fear if you shook a dog-whip at 'em. But they know you're forbidden to do that, so they conspire to make your life a burden to you. My District's worked by some man at Darjiling, on the strength of a pleader's false reports. Oh, it's a heavenly place!"

Otis Yeere laughed bitterly.

"There's not the least necessity that you should stay in it. Why do you?"

"Because I must. How'm I to get out of it?"

"How! In a hundred and fifty ways. If there weren't so many people on the road, I'd like to box your ears. Ask, my dear sir, *ask!* Look! There is young Hexarly with six years' service and half your talents. He asked for what he wanted, and he got it. See, down by the Convent! There's McArthurson who has come to his present position by asking—sheer, downright asking—after he had pushed himself out of the rank and file. One man is as good as another in your service—believe me. I've seen Simla for more seasons than I care to think about. Do you suppose men are chosen for appointments because of their special fitness *beforehand?* You have all passed a high test—what do you call it?—in the beginning, and, excepting the three or four who have gone altogether to the bad, you can all work. Asking does the rest. Call it cheek, call it insolence, call it anything you like, but *ask!* Men argue—yes, I know what men say—that a man, by the mere audacity of his request, *must* have some good in him. A weak man doesn't say: 'Give me this and that.' He whines: 'Why haven't I been given this and that?' If you were in the Army, I should say learn to spin plates or

play a tambourine with your toes. As it is—*ask!*
You belong to a Service that ought to be able to
command the Channel fleet, or set a leg at twenty
minutes' notice, and *yet* you hesitate over asking
to escape from the squashy green district where
you *admit* you are not master. Drop the Bengal
Government altogether. Even Darjiling is a little
out-of-the-way hole. I was there once, and the
rents were extortionate. Assert yourself. Get
the Government of India to take you over. Try
to get on the Frontier, where *every* man has a
grand chance if he can trust himself. *Go* somewhere! *Do* something! You have twice the wits
and three times the presence of the men up here,
and—and"—Mrs. Hauksbee paused for breath;
then continued—"and in *any* way you look at it,
you *ought* to. *You* who could go so far!"

"I don't know," said Yeere, rather taken aback
by the unexpected eloquence. "I haven't such
a good opinion of myself."

It was not strictly Platonic, but it was Policy.
Mrs. Hauksbee laid her hand lightly upon the
ungloved paw that rested on the turned-back 'rickshaw hood, and, looking the man full in the face,
said tenderly, almost too tenderly: "*I* believe in
you if you mistrust yourself. Is that enough, my
friend?"

"It is enough," answered Otis, very solemnly.

He was silent for a long time, redreaming the
dreams that he had dreamed eight years ago, but
through them all ran, as sheet-lightning through

a golden cloud, the light of Mrs. Hauksbee's violet eyes.

Curious and impenetrable are the mazes of Simla life—the only existence in this desolate land worth the living. Gradually it went abroad among men and women, in the pauses between dance, play, and Gymkhana, that Otis Yeere, the man with the newly lit light of self-confidence in his eyes, had "done something decent" in the wilds whence he came. He had brought an erring Municipality to reason, appropriated the funds on his own responsibility, and saved the lives of hundreds. He knew more about the Gullals than any living man. Had a vast knowledge of the aboriginal tribes; was, in spite of his juniority, the greatest authority on the aboriginal Gullals. No one quite knew who or what the Gullals were till The Mussuck, who had been calling on Mrs. Hauksbee, and prided himself upon picking people's brains, explained they were a tribe of ferocious hill-men, somewhere near Sikkim, whose friendship even the Great Indian Empire would find it worth her while to secure. Now we know that Otis Yeere had showed Mrs. Hauksbee his M. S. notes of six years' standing on these same Gullals. He had told her, too, how, sick and shaken with the fever their negligence had bred, crippled by the loss of his pet clerk, and savagely angry at the desolation of his charge, he had once damned the collective eyes of his "intelligent local board" for a set of haramzadas. Which act of "brutal and tyrannous oppression" won him a Reprimand Royal from the Bengal Government; but in the anecdote as amended for Northern consumption, we find no record of this. Hence we are forced to conclude that Mrs. Hauksbee "edited" his reminiscences before sowing them in idle ears, ready, as she well knew, to exaggerate good or evil. And Otis Yeere bore himself as befitted the hero of many tales.

"You can talk to *me* when you don't fall into a brown study. Talk now, and talk your brightest and best," said Mrs. Hauksbee.

Otis needed no spur. Look to a man who has the counsel of a woman of or above the world to back him. So long as he keeps his head, he can meet both sexes on equal ground—an advantage never intended by Providence, who fashioned Man on one day and Woman on another, in sign that neither should know more than a very little of the other's life. Such a man goes far, or, the counsel being withdrawn, collapses suddenly while his world seeks the reason.

Generaled by Mrs. Hauksbee, who, again, had all Mrs. Mallowe's wisdom at her disposal, proud of himself, and, in the end, believing in himself because he was believed in, Otis Yeere stood ready for any fortune that might befall, certain that it would be good. He would fight for his own hand, and intended that this second struggle should lead to better issue than the first helpless surrender of the bewildered 'Stunt.

What might have happened, it is impossible to say. This lamentable thing befell, bred directly by a statement of Mrs. Hauksbee that she would spend the next season in Darjiling.

"Are you certain of that?" said Otis Yeere.

"Quite. We're writing about a house now."

Otis Yeere "stopped dead," as Mrs. Hauksbee put it in discussing the relapse with Mrs. Mallowe.

"He has behaved," she said, angrily, "just like Captain Kerrington's pony—only Otis is a donkey —at the last Gymkhana. Planted his forefeet and refused to go on another step. Polly, my man's going to disappoint me. What shall I do?"

As a rule, Mrs. Mallowe does not approve of staring, but on this occasion she opened her eyes to the utmost.

"You have mamaged cleverly so far," she said. "Speak to him, and ask him what he means."

"I will—at to-night's dance."

"No—o, not at a dance," said Mrs. Mallowe, cautiously. "Men are never themselves quite at dances. Better wait till to-morrow morning."

"Nonsense. If he's going to revert in this insane way, there isn't a day to lose. Are you going? No! Then sit up for me, there's a dear. I shan't stay longer than supper under any circumstances."

Mrs. Mallowe waited through the evening, looking long and earnestly into the fire, and sometimes smiling to herself.

* * * * * * *

"Oh! oh! oh! The man's an idiot! A raving, positive idiot! I'm sorry I ever saw him!"

Mrs. Hauksbee burst into Mrs. Mallowe's house, at midnight, almost in tears.

"What in the world has happened?" said Mrs. Mallowe, but her eyes showed that she had guessed an answer.

"Happened! Everything has happened! He was there. I went to him and said: 'Now, what does this nonsense mean?' Don't laugh, dear, I can't bear it. But you know what I mean I said. Then it was a square, and I sat it out with him and wanted an explanation, and *he* said—Oh! I haven't patience with such idiots! You know what I said about going to Darjiling next year? It doesn't matter to me *where* I go. I'd have changed the Station and lost the rent to have saved this. He said, in so many words, that he wasn't going to try to work up any more, because—because he would be shifted into a province away from Darjiling, and his own District, where these creatures are, is within a day's journey——"

"Ah—hh!" said Mrs. Mallowe, in a tone of one who has successfully tracked an obscure word through a large dictionary.

"Did you ever *hear* of anything so mad—so absurd? And he had the ball at his feet. He had

only to kick it! I would have made him anything!
Anything in the wide world. He could have gone
to the world's end. I would have helped him. I
made him, didn't I, Polly? Didn't I create that
man? Doesn't he owe everything to me? And to
reward me, just when everything was nicely arranged, by this *lunacy* that spoiled everything!"

"Very few men understand devotion thoroughly."

"Oh, Polly, *don't* laugh at me! I give men up
from this hour. I could have killed him then and
there. What *right* had this man—this *Thing* I
had picked out of his filthy paddy-fields—to make
love to me?"

"He did that, did he?"

"He did. I don't remember half he said, I
was so angry. Oh, but such a funny thing happened! I can't help laughing at it now, though I
felt nearly ready to cry with rage. He raved,
and I stormed—I'm afraid we must have made
an awful noise in our kala juggah. Protect my
character, dear, if it's all over Simla by to-morrow
—and then he bobbed forward in the middle of
this insanity—and I *firmly* believe the man's de-
mented—and kissed me."

"Morals above reproach," purred Mrs. Mallowe.

"So they were—so they are! It was the most
absurd kiss. I don't believe he'd ever kissed a
woman in his life before. I threw my head back,
and it was a sort of slidy, pecking dab, just on

the end of the chin—here." Mrs. Hauksbee tapped her rather masculine chin with her fan. "Then, of course, I was *furiously* angry, and told him that he was no gentleman, and I was sorry I'd ever met him, and so on. He was crushed so easily that I couldn't be *very* angry. Then I came away straight to you."

"Was this before or after supper?"

"Oh! before—oceans before. Isn't it perfectly disgusting?"

"Let me think. I withhold judgment till to-morrow. Morning brings counsel."

But morning brought only a servant with a dainty bouquet of Annandale roses for Mrs. Hauksbee to wear at the dance at Viceregal Lodge that night.

"He doesn't seem to be *very* penitent," said Mrs. Mallowe. "What's the *billet-doux* in the center?"

Mrs. Hauksbee opened the neatly folded note —another accomplishment that she had taught Otis—read it, and groaned tragically.

"Last wreck of a feeble intellect! Poetry! Is it his own, do you think? Oh, that I ever built my hopes on such a maudlin idiot!"

"No. It's a quotation from Mrs. Browning, and, in view of the facts of the case, as Jack says, uncommonly well chosen. Listen:

"Sweet, thou hast trod on a heart—
    Pass! There's a world full of men:

And women as fair as thou art,
  Must do such things now and then.

"Thou only hast stepped unaware—
  Malice not one can impute;
And why should a heart have been there.
  In the way of a fair woman's foot?"

"I didn't—I didn't—I didn't!" said Mrs.
Hauksbee, angrily, her eyes filling with tears;
"there was no malice at all. Oh, it's *too* vexa-
tious!"

"You've misunderstood the compliment," said
Mrs. Mallowe. "He clears you completely, and—
ahem!—I should think by this, that *he* has cleared
completely, too. My experience of men is that
when they begin to quote poetry, they are going to
flit. Like swans singing before they die, you
know."

"Polly, you take my sorrows in a most unfeeling
way."

"Do I? Is it so terrible? If he's hurt your
vanity, I should say that you've done a certain
amount of damage to his heart."

"Oh, you can never tell about a *man!*" said
Mrs. Hauksbee, with deep scorn.

*   *   *   *   *   *   *

Reviewing the matter as an impartial outsider,
it strikes me that I'm about the only person who
has profited by the education of Otis Yeere. It
comes to twenty-seven pages and bittock.

AT THE PIT'S MOUTH

Men say it was a stolen tide—
  The Lord that sent it He knows all,
But in mine ear will aye abide
  The message that the bells let fall,
And awesome bells they were to me,
That in the dark rang, "Enderby."
—*Jean Ingelow.*

ONCE upon a time there was a Man and his Wife and a Tertium Quid.

All three were unwise, but the Wife was the unwisest. The Man should have looked after his Wife, who should have avoided the Tertium Quid, who, again, should have married a wife of his own, after clean and open flirtations, to which nobody can possibly object, round Jakko or Observatory Hill. When you see a young man with his pony in a white lather, and his hat on the back of his head, flying down-hill at fifteen miles an hour to meet a girl who will be properly surprised to meet him, you naturally approve of that young man, and you wish him Staff appointments, and take an interest in his welfare, and, as the proper time comes, give him sugar-tongs or side-saddles, according to your means and generosity.

The Tertium Quid flew down-hill on horseback, but it was to meet the Man's Wife; and when he flew up-hill it was for the same end. The Man was in the Plains, earning money for his Wife to spend on dresses and four-hundred-rupee bracelets, and inexpensive luxuries of that kind. He worked very hard, and sent her a letter or postcard daily. She also wrote to him daily, and said that she was longing for him to come up to Simla. The Tertium Quid used to lean over her shoulder and laugh as she wrote the notes. Then the two would ride to the post-office together.

Now, Simla is a strange place, and its customs are peculiar; nor is any man who has not spent at least ten seasons there qualified to pass judgment on circumstantial evidence, which is the most untrustworthy in the Courts. For these reasons, and for others which need not appear, I decline to state positively whether there was anything irretrievably wrong in the relations between the Man's Wife and the Tertium Quid. If there was, and hereon you must form your own opinion, it was the Man's Wife's fault. She was kittenish in her manners, wearing generally an air of soft and fluffy innocence. But she was deadly learned and evil-instructed; now and again, when the mask dropped, men saw this, shuddered, and—almost drew back. Men are occasionally particular, and the least particular are always the most exacting.

Simla is eccentric in its fashion of treating friendships. Certain attachments which have set and crystallized through half a dozen seasons acquire almost the sanctity of the marriage bond, and are revered as such. Again, certain attachments equally old, and, to all appearance, equally venerable, never seem to win any recognized official status; while a chance-sprung acquaintance, not two months old, steps into the place which by right belongs to the senor. There is no law reducible to print which regulates these affairs.

Some people have a gift which secures them infinite toleration, and others have not. The Man's Wife had not. If she looked over the garden wall, for instance, women taxed her with stealing their husbands. She complained pathetically that she was not allowed to choose her own friends. When she put up her big white muff to her lips, and gazed over it and under her eyebrows at you as she said this thing, you felt that she had been infamously misjudged, and that all the other women's instincts were all wrong; which was absurd. She was not allowed to own the Tertium Quid in peace; and was so strangely constructed that she would not have enjoyed peace had she been so permitted. She preferred some intrigue to cloak even her most commonplace actions.

After two months of riding, first round Jakko, then Elysium, then Summer Hill, then Observatory Hill, then under Jutogh, and lastly up and down the Cart Road as far as the Tara Devi gap in the dusk, she said to the Tertium Quid: "Frank, people say we are too much together, and people are so horrid."

The Tertium Quid pulled his mustache, and replied that horrid people were unworthy of the consideration of nice people.

"But they have done more than talk—they have written—written to my hubby—I'm sure of it," said the Man's Wife; and she pulled a letter from her husband out of her saddle-pocket and gave it to the Tertium Quid.

It was an honest letter, written by an honest man, then stewing in the Plains on two hundred rupees a month (for he allowed his wife eight hundred and fifty), and in a silk banian and cotton trousers. It is said that, perhaps, she had not thought of the unwisdom of allowing her name to be so generally coupled with the Tertium Quid's; that she was too much of a child to understand the dangers of that sort of thing; that he, her husband, was the last man in the world to interfere jealously with her little amusements and interests, but that it would be better were she to drop the Tertium Quid quietly and for her husband's sake. The letter was sweetened with many pretty little pet names, and it amused the Tertium Quid considerably. He and She laughed over it, so that you could see their shoulders shaking while the horses slouched along side by side.

Their conversation was not worth reporting. The upshot of it was that, next day, no one saw the Man's Wife and the Tertium Quid together. They had both gone down to the Cemetery, which is only visited officially by the inhabitants of Simla.

A Simla funeral with the clergyman riding, the

mourners riding, and the coffin creaking as it swings between the bearers, is one of the most depressing things on this earth, particularly when the procession passes under the wet, dank dip beneath the Rockcliffe Hotel, where the sun is shut out, and all the hill streams are wailing and weeping together as they go down the valleys.

Occasionally, folk tend the graves; but we in India shift and are transferred so often that, at the end of the second year, the Dead have no friends—only acquaintances who are far too busy amusing themselves up the hill to attend to old partners. The idea of using a Cemetery as a rendezvous is distinctly a feminine one. A man would have said simply: "Let people talk. We'll go down the Mall." A woman is made differently, especially if she be such a woman as the Man's Wife. She and the Tertium Quid enjoyed each other's society among the graves of men and women they had known and danced with aforetime.

They used to take a big horse-blanket and sit on the grass a little to the left of the lower end, where there is a dip in the ground, and where the occupied graves die out and ready-made ones are not ready. Any self-respecting Indian Cemetery keeps half a dozen graves permanently open for contingencies and incidental wear and tear. In the Hills these are more usually baby's size, because children who come up weakened and sick from the Plains often succumb to the effects of the Rains in the Hills, or get pneumonia from their ayahs taking them through damp pine-woods after the sun has set. In Cantonments, of course, the man's size is more in request, these arrangements varying with the climate and population.

One day when the Man's Wife and the Tertium Quid had just arrived in the Cemetery, they saw some coolies breaking ground. They had marked out a full-sized grave, and the Tertium Quid asked them whether any Sahib was sick. They said that they did not know; but it was an order that they should dig a Sahib's grave.

"Work away," said Tertium Quid, "and let's see how it's done."

The coolies worked away, and the Man's Wife and the Tertium Quid watched and talked for a couple of hours while the grave was being deepened. Then a coolie, taking the earth in baskets as it was thrown up, jumped over the grave.

"That's queer," said the Tertium Quid. "Where's my ulster?"

"What's queer?" said the Man's Wife.

"I have got a chill down my back—just as if a goose had walked over my grave."

"Why do you look at the horror, then?" said the Man's Wife. "Let us go."

The Tertium Quid stood at the head of the grave, and stared without answering for a space. Then he said, dropping a pebble down: "It is nasty—and cold: horribly cold. I don't think I shall come to the Cemetery any more. I don't think grave-digging is cheerful."

The two talked and agreed that the Cemetery was depressing. They also arranged for a ride next day out from the Cemetery through the Mashobra Tunnel up to Fagoo and back, because all the world was going to a garden-party at Viceregal Lodge, and all the people of Mashobra would go, too.

Coming up the Cemetery road, the Tertium Quid's horse tried to bolt up-hill, being tired with standing so long, and strained a back sinew.

"I shall have to take the mare to-morrow," said the Tertium Quid, "and she will stand nothing heavier than a snaffle."

They made their arrangements to meet in the Cemetery, after allowing all the Mashobra people to pass into Simla. That night it rained heavily, and, next day, when the Tertium Quid came to the trysting-place, he saw that the new grave had a foot of water in it, the ground being a tough and sour clay.

"Jove! That looks beastly," said the Tertium Quid. "Fancy being boarded up and dropped into that well!"

They then started off to Fagoo, the mare playing with the snaffle and picking her way as though she were shod with satin, and the sun shining divinely. The road below Mashobra to Fagoo is officially styled the Himalayan-Thibet Road; but in spite of its name it is not much more than six feet wide in most places, and the drop into the valley below between one and two thousand feet.

"Now we're going to Thibet," said the Man's Wife, merrily, as the horses drew near to Fagoo. She was riding on the cliff-side.

"Into Thibet," said the Tertium Quid, "ever so far from people who say horrid things, and hubbys who write stupid letters. With you—to the end of the world!"

A coolie carrying a log of wood came round a corner, and the mare went wide to avoid him—forefeet in and hunches out, as a sensible mare should go.

"To the world's end," said the Man's Wife, and looked unspeakable things over her near shoulder at the Tertium Quid.

He was smiling, but, while she looked, the smile froze stiff, as it were, on his face, and changed to a nervous grin—the sort of grin men wear when they are not quite easy in their saddles. The mare seemed to be sinking by the stern, and her nostrils cracked while she was trying to realize what was happening. The rain of the previous night had rotted the drop-side of the Himalayan-Thibet Road, and it was giving way under her. "What are you doing?" said the Man's Wife. The Tertium Quid gave no answer. He grinned nervously and set his spurs into the mare, who rapped with her forefeet on the road, and the struggle began. The Man's Wife screamed: "Oh, Frank, get off!"

But the Tertium Quid was glued to the saddle —his face blue and white—and he looked into

the Man's Wife's eyes. Then the Man's Wife
clutched at the mare's head and caught her by the
nose instead of the bridle. The brute threw up
her head and went down with a scream, the Tertium Quid upon her, and the nervous grin still
set on his face.

The Man's Wife heard the tinkle-tinkle of little
stones and loose earth falling off the road-way,
and the sliding roar of the man and horse going
down. Then everything was quiet, and she called
on Frank to leave his mare and walk up. But
Frank did not answer. He was underneath the
mare, nine hundred feet below, spoiling a patch
of Indian corn.

As the revelers came back from Viceregal
Lodge in the mists of the evening, they met a
temporarily insane woman, on a temporarily
mad horse, swinging round the corners, with her
eyes and her mouth open, and her head like the
head of a Medusa. She was stopped by a man
at the risk of his life, and taken out of the saddle,
a limp heap, and put on the bank to explain herself. This wasted twenty minutes, and then she
was sent home in a lady's 'rickshaw, still with
her mouth open and her hands picking at her rid-
ing-gloves.

She was in bed for the following three days,
which were rainy; so she missed attending the
funeral of the Tertium Quid, who was lowered
into eighteen inches of water, instead of the
twelve to which he had at first objected.

A WAYSIDE COMEDY

BECAUSE to every purpose there is time and judgment;
therefore the misery of man is great upon him. —*Eccl*. viii. 6.

FATE and the Government of India have turned
the Station of Kashima into a prison; and, because there is no help for the poor souls who are
now lying there in torment, I write this story,
praying that the Government of India may be
moved to scatter the European population to the
four winds.

Kashima is bounded on all sides by the rock-
tipped circle of the Dosehri hills.   In Spring,
it is ablaze with roses; in Summer, the roses die
and the hot winds blow from the hills; in Autumn,
the white mists from the jhils cover the place as
with water, and in Winter the frosts nip everything young and tender to earth level.   There is
but one view in Kashima—that of a stretch of
perfectly flat pasture and plow-land, running up
to the gray-blue scrub of the Dosehri hills.

There are no amusements except snipe and
tiger shooting; but the tigers have long since
been hunted from their lairs in the rock-caves,
and the snipe only come once a year.   Narkarra
—one hundred and forty-three miles by road—is
the nearest station to Kashima.   But Kashima

never goes to Narkarra, where there are at least twelve English people. It stays within the circle of the Dosehri hills.

All Kashima acquits Mrs. Vansuythen of any intention to do harm; but all Kashima knows that she, and she alone, brought about their pain.

Boulte, the engineer, Mrs. Boulte and Captain Kurrell know this. They are the English population of Kashima, if we except Major Vansuythen, who is of no importance whatever, and Mrs. Vansuythen, who is the most important of all.

You must remember, though you will not understand, that all laws weaken in a small and hidden community where there is no public opinion. If the Israelites had been only a ten-tent camp of gypsies, their Headman would never have taken the trouble to climb a hill and bring down the lithographed edition of the Decalogue, and a great deal of trouble would have been avoided. When a man is absolutely alone in a Station, he runs a certain risk of falling into evil ways. This risk is multiplied by every addition to the population up to twelve—the Jury number. After that, fear and consequent restraint begin, and human action becomes less grotesquely jerky.

There was deep peace in Kashima till Mrs. Vansuythen arrived. She was a charming woman, every one said so everywhere; and she charmed every one. In spite of this, or, perhaps, because of this, since Fate is so maliciously perverse, she cared only for one man, and he was Major Vansuythen. Had she been plain or stupid, this matter would have been intelligible to Kashima. But she was a fair woman, with very still gray eyes, the color of a lake just before the light of the sun touches it. No man who had seen those eyes could, later on, explain what fashion of woman she was to look upon. The eyes dazzled him. Her own sex said that she was "not bad looking, but spoiled by pretending to be so grave." And yet her gravity was natural. It was not her habit to smile. She merely went through life, looking at those who passed; and the women objected, while the men fell down and worshiped.

She knows and is deeply sorry for the evil she has done to Kashima; but Major Vansuythen can not understand why Mrs. Boulte does not drop in to afternoon tea at least three times a week. "When there are only two women in one Station, they ought to see a great deal of each other," says Major Vansuythen.

Long and long before ever Mrs. Vansuythen came out of those far-away places where there is society and amusement, Kurrell had discovered that Mrs. Boulte was the one woman in the world for him, and—you dare not blame them. Kashima was as out of the world as Heaven or the other place, and the Dosehri hills kept their secret well. Boulte had no concern in the matter. He was in camp for a fortnight at a time. He was a hard, heavy man, and neither Mrs. Boulte nor Kurrell pitied him. They had all Kashima and each other for their very, very own; and Kashima was the Garden of Eden in those days. When Boulte returned from his wanderings he would slap Kurrell between the shoulders and call him "old fellow," and the three would dine together. Kashima was happy then, when the judgment of God seemed almost as distant as Narkarra or the railway that ran down to the sea. But the Government sent Major Vansuythen to Kashima, and with him came his wife.

The etiquette of Kashima is much the same as that of a desert island. When a stranger is cast away there, all hands go down to the shore to make him welcome. Kashima assembled at the masonry platform close to the Narkarra Road, and spread tea for the Vansuythens. That ceremony was reckoned a formal call, and made them free of the Station, its rights and privileges. When the Vansuythens were settled down, they gave a tiny house-warming to all Kashima; and that made Kashima free of their house, according to the immemorial usage of the Station.

Then the Rains came, when no one could go into camp, and the Narkarra Road was washed away by the Kasun River, and in the cup-like pas-

tures of Kashima the cattle waded knee-deep.
The clouds dropped down from the Dosehri hills
and covered everything.

At the end of the Rains, Boulte's manner toward his wife changed and became demonstra-
tively affectionate. They had been married
twelve years, and the change startled Mrs.
Boulte, who hated her husband with the hate of
a woman who has met with nothing but kindness
from her mate, and, in the teeth of this kindness,
has done him a great wrong. Moreover, she had
her own trouble to fight with—her watch to keep
over her own property, Kurrell. For two months
the Rains had hidden the Dosehri hills and many
other things beside; but, when they lifted, they
showed Mrs. Boulte that her man among men, her
Ted—for she called him Ted in the old days when
Boulte was out of earshot—was slipping the links
of the allegiance.

"The Vansuythen Woman has taken him,"
Mrs. Boulte said to herself; and when Boulte was
away, wept over her belief, in the face of the
over-vehement blandishments of Ted. Sorrow
in Kashima is as fortunate as Love, in that there
is nothing to weaken it save the flight of Time.
Mrs. Boulte had never breathed her suspicion to
Kurrell, because she was not certain; and her nature led her to be very certain before she took
steps in any direction. That is why she behaved
as she did.

Boulte came into the house one evening, and

leaned against the door-post of the drawing-
room, chewing his mustache. Mrs. Boulte was
putting some flowers into a vase. There is a pretense of civilization even in Kashima.

"Little woman," said Boulte, quietly, "do you
care for me?"

"Immensely," said she, with a laugh. "Can you
ask it?"

"But I'm serious," said Boulte. "Do you care
for me?"

Mrs. Boulte dropped the flowers, and turned
round quickly. "Do you want an honest answer?"

"Ye-es; I've asked for it."

Mrs. Boulte spoke in a low, even voice for five
minutes, very distinctly, that there might be no
misunderstanding her meaning. When Samson
broke the pillars of Gaza, he did a little thing,
and one not to be compared to the deliberate pulling down of a woman's homestead about her own
ears. There was no wise female friend to advise
Mrs. Boulte, the singularly cautious wife, to hold
her hand. She struck at Boulte's heart, because
her own was sick with suspicion of Kurrell, and
worn out with the long strain of watching alone
through the Rains. There was no plan or purpose in her speaking. The sentences made themselves; and Boulte listened, leaning against the
door-post with his hands in his pockets. When
all was over, and Mrs. Boulte began to breathe
through her nose before breaking out into tears,

he laughed and stared straight in front of him at the Dosehri hills.

"Is that all?" he said. "Thanks; I only wanted to know, you know."

"What are you going to do?" said the woman, between her sobs.

"Do! Nothing. What should I do? Kill Kurrell or send you home, or apply for leave to get a divorce? It's two days' dâk into Narkarra." He laughed again and went on: "I'll tell you what *you* can do. You can ask Kurrell to dinner to-morrow—no, on Thursday; that will allow you time to pack—and you can bolt with him. I give you my word, I won't follow."

He took up his helmet and went out of the room, and Mrs. Boulte sat till the moonlight streaked the floor, thinking and thinking and thinking. She had done her best upon the spur of the moment to pull the house down; but it would not fall. Moreover, she could not understand her husband, and she was afraid. Then the folly of her useless truthfulness struck her, and she was ashamed to write to Kurrell, saying: "I have gone mad and told everything. My husband says that I am free to elope with you. Get a dâk for Thursday and we will fly after dinner." There was a cold-bloodedness about that procedure which did not appeal to her. So she sat still in her own house and thought.

At dinner-time Boulte came back from his walk, white and worn and haggard, and the woman was touched at his distress. As the evening wore on, she muttered some expression of sorrow, something approaching to contrition. Boulte came out of a brown study, and said: "Oh, *that!* I wasn't thinking about that. By the way, what does Kurrell say to the elopement?"

"I haven't seen him," said Mrs. Boulte. "Good God! is that all?"

But Boulte was not listening, and her sentence ended in a gulp.

The next day brought no comfort to Mrs. Boulte, for Kurrell did not appear, and the new life that she, in the five minutes' madness of the previous evening, had hoped to build out of the ruins of the old, seemed to be no nearer.

Boulte ate his breakfast, advised her to see her Arab pony fed in the veranda, and went out. The morning wore through, and at midday the tension became unendurable. Mrs. Boulte could not cry. She had finished her crying in the night, and now she did not want to be left alone. Perhaps the Vansuythen Woman would talk to her; and, since talking opens the heart, perhaps there might be some comfort to be found in her company. She was the only other woman in the Station.

In Kashima there are no regular calling hours. Every one can drop in upon every one else at pleasure. Mrs. Boulte put on a big terai hat, and walked across to the Vansuythens' house to borrow last week's "Queen." The two compounds touched, and instead of going up the drive she crossed through the gap in the cactus-hedge entering the house from the back. As she passed through the dining-room, she heard, behind the purdah that cloaked the drawing-room door, her husband's voice, saying:

"But on my Honor! On my Soul and Honor, I tell you she doesn't care for me. She told me so last night. I would have told you then if Vansuythen hadn't been with you. If it is for *her* sake that you'll have nothing to say to me, you can make your mind easy. It's Kurrell—"

"What?" said Mrs. Vansuythen, with an hysterical little laugh. "Kurrell! Oh, it can't be! You two must have made some horrible mistake. Perhaps you—you lost your temper, or misunderstood, or something. Things *can't* be as wrong as you say."

Mrs. Vansuythen had shifted her defense to avoid the man's pleading, and was desperately trying to keep him to a side-issue.

"There must be some mistake," she insisted, "and it can be all put right again."

Boulte laughed grimly.

"It can't be Captain Kurrell! He told me that he had never taken the least—the least interest in your wife, Mr. Boulte. Oh, *do* listen! He said he had not. He swore he had not," said Mrs. Vansuythen.

The purdah rustled, and the speech was cut short by the entry of a little, thin woman, with big rings round her eyes. Mrs. Vansuythen stood up with a gasp.

"What was that you said?" asked Mrs. Boulte. "Never mind that man. What did Ted say to you? What did he say to you? What did he say to you?"

Mrs. Vansuythen sat down helplessly on the sofa, overborne by the trouble of her questioner.

"He said—I can't remember exactly what he said—but I understood him to say—that is . . . But, really, Mrs. Boulte, isn't it rather a strange question?"

"*Will* you tell me what he said?" repeated Mrs. Boulte. Even a tiger will fly before a bear robbed of her whelps, and Mrs. Vansuythen was only an ordinarily good woman. She began in a sort of desperation: "Well, he said that he never cared for you at all, and, of course, there was not the least reason why he should have, and—and—that was all."

"You said he *swore* he had not cared for me. Was that true?"

"Yes," said Mrs. Vansuythen, very softly.

Mrs. Boulte wavered for an instant where she stood, and then fell forward fainting.

"What did I tell you?" said Boulte, as though the conversation had been unbroken. "You can see for yourself. She cares for *him*." The light began to break into his dull mind, and he went on: "And he—what was *he* saying to you?"

But Mrs. Vansuythen, with no heart for ex-

planations or impassioned protestations, was
kneeling over Mrs. Boulte.

"Oh, you brute!" she cried. "Are *all* men like
this? Help me to get her into my room—and her
face is cut against the table. Oh, *will* you be
quiet, and help me to carry her? I hate you, and
I hate Captain Kurrell. Lift her up carefully,
and now—go! Go away!"

Boulte carried his wife into Mrs. Vansuythen's
bedroom, and departed before the storm of that
lady's wrath and disgust, impenitent and burning
with jealousy. Kurrell had been making love to
Mrs. Vansuythen—would do Vansuythen as
great a wrong as he had done Boulte, who caught
himself considering whether Mrs. Vansuythen
would faint if she discovered that the man she
loved had foresworn her.

In the middle of these meditations, Kurrell
came cantering along the road and pulled up with
a cheery: "Good-mornin'. 'Been mashing Mrs.
Vansuythen as usual, eh? Bad thing for a sober,
married man, that. What will Mrs. Boulte say?"

Boulte raised his head and said, slowly:

"Oh, you liar!" Kurrell's face changed.

"What's that?" he asked quickly.

"Nothing much," said Boulte. "Has my wife
told you that you two are free to go off whenever
you please? She has been good enough to explain the situation to me. You've been a true
friend to me, Kurrell—old man—haven't you?"

Kurrell groaned, and tried to frame some sort

of idiotic sentence about being willing to give "satisfaction." But his interest in the woman was dead, had died out in the Rains, and, mentally, he was abusing her for her amazing indiscretion. It would have been so easy to have broken off the *liaison* gently and by degrees, and now he was saddled with . . . Boulte's voice recalled him.

"I don't think I should get any satisfaction from killing you, and I'm pretty sure you'd get none from killing me."

Then in a querulous tone, ludicrously disproportioned to his wrongs, Boulte added:

" 'Seems rather a pity that you haven't the decency to keep to the woman, now you've got her. You've been a true friend to *her,* too, haven't you?"

Kurrell stared long and gravely. The situation was getting beyond him.

"What do you mean?" he said.

Boulte answered, more to himself than the questioner: "My wife came over to Mrs. Vansuythen's just now; and it seems you'd been telling Mrs. Vansuythen that you'd never cared for Emma. I suppose you lied, as usual. What had Mrs. Vansuythen to do with you, or you with her? Try to speak the truth for once in a way."

Kurrell took the double insult without wincing, and replied by another question.

"Go on. What happened?"

"Emma fainted," said Boulte, simply. "But,

look here, what had you been saying to Mrs. Vansuythen?"

Kurrell laughed. Mrs. Boulte had, with unbridled tongue, made havoc of his plans; and he could at least retaliate by hurting the man in whose eyes he was humiliated and shown dishonorable.

"Said to her? What *does* a man tell a lie like that for? I suppose I said pretty much what you've said, unless I'm a good deal mistaken."

"I spoke the truth," said Boulte, again more to himself than Kurrell. "Emma told me she hated me. She has no right in me."

"No! I suppose not. You're only her husband, y'know. And what did Mrs. Vansuythen say after you had laid your disengaged heart at her feet?"

Kurrell felt almost virtuous as he put the question.

"I don't think that matters," Boulte replied; "and it doesn't concern you."

"But it does! I tell you it does," began Kurrell, shamelessly.

His sentence was cut by a roar of laughter from Boulte's lips. Kurrell was silent for an instant, and then he, too, laughed—laughed long and loudly, rocking in his saddle. It was an unpleasant sound—the mirthless mirth of these men on the long, white line of the Narkarra Road. There were no strangers in Kashima, or they might have thought that captivity within the

Dosehri hills had driven half the European population mad. The laughter stopped abruptly. Kurrell was the first to speak.

"Well, what are you going to do?"

Boulte looked up the road, and at the hills. "Nothing," said he, quietly. "What's the use? It's too ghastly for anything. We must let the old life go on. I can only call you a hound and a liar, and I can't go on calling you names forever. Besides which, I don't feel that I'm much better. We can't get out of this place, y'know. What is there to do?"

Kurrell looked round the rat-pit of Kashima, and made no reply. The injured husband took up the wondrous tale.

"Ride on, and speak to Emma if you want to. God knows *I* don't care what you do."

He walked forward, and left Kurrell gazing blankly after him. Kurrell did not ride on either to see Mrs. Boulte or Mrs. Vansuythen. He sat in his saddle and thought, while his pony grazed by the road-side.

The whirr of approaching wheels roused him. Mrs. Vansuythen was driving home Mrs. Boulte, white and wan, with a cut on her forehead.

"Stop, please," said Mrs. Boulte. "I want to speak to Ted."

Mrs. Vansuythen obeyed, but as Mrs. Boulte leaned forward, putting her hand upon the splash-board of the dog-cart, Kurrell spoke.

"I've seen your husband, Mrs. Boulte."

There was no necessity for any further explanation. The man's eyes were fixed, not upon Mrs. Boulte, but her companion. Mrs. Boulte saw the look.

"Speak to him!" she pleaded, turning to the woman at her side. "Oh, speak to him! Tell him what you told me just now. Tell him you hate him! Tell him you hate him!"

She bent forward and wept bitterly, while the sais, decorously impassive, went forward to hold the horse. Mrs. Vansuythen turned scarlet and dropped the rein. She wished to be no party to such an unholy explanation.

"I've nothing to do with it," she began, coldly; but Mrs. Boulte's sobs overcame her, and she addressed herself to the man. "I don't know what I am to say, Captain Kurrell. I don't know what I can call you. I think you've—you've behaved abominably, and she has cut her forehead terribly against the table."

"It doesn't hurt. It isn't anything," said Mrs. Boulte, feebly. *"That* doesn't matter. Tell him what you told me. Say you don't care for him. Oh, Ted, *won't* you believe her?"

"Mrs. Boulte has made me understand that you were—that you were fond of her once upon a time," went on Mrs. Vansuythen.

"Well!" said Kurrell, brutally. "It seems to me that Mrs. Boulte had better be fond of her own husband first."

"Stop!" said Mrs. Vansuythen. "Hear me

first. I don't care—I don't want to know anything about you and Mrs. Boulte; but I want *you*
to know that I hate you; that I think you are a
cur, and that I'll never, *never* speak to you again.
Oh, I don't dare to say what I think of you, you
. . . man! *Sais, gorah ko jane do.*"

"I want to speak to Ted," moaned Mrs. Boulte;
but the dog-cart rattled on, and Kurrell was left
on the road, shamed, and boiling with wrath
against Mrs. Boulte.

He waited till Mrs. Vansuythen was driving
back to her own house, and, she being freed from
the embarrassment of Mrs. Boulte's presence,
learned for the second time a truthful opinion of
himself and his actions.

In the evenings, it was the wont of all Kashima to meet at the platform on the Narkarra
Road, to drink tea, and discuss the trivialities of
the day.   Major Vansuythen and his wife found
themselves alone at the gathering-place for almost the first time in their remembrance; and the
cheery Major, in the teeth of his wife's remark-
ably reasonable suggestion that the rest of the
Station might be sick, insisted upon driving round
to the two bungalows and unearthing the population.

"Sitting in the twilight!" said he, with great
indignation, to the Boultes.   "That'll never do!
Hang it all, we're one family here!   You *must*
come out, and so must Kurrell.   I'll make him
bring his banjo."

So great is the power of honest simplicity and
a good digestion over guilty consciences that all
Kashima did turn out, even down to the banjo;
and the Major embraced the company in one ex-
pansive grin. As he grinned, Mrs. Vansuythen
raised her eyes for an instant and looked at
Kashima. Her meaning was clear. Major Vansuythen would never know anything. He was to
be the outsider in that happy family whose cage
was the Dosehri hills.

"You're singing villainously out of tune, Kurrell," said the Major, truthfully. "Pass me that
banjo."

And he sung in excruciating-wise till the stars
came out and Kashima went to dinner.

*   *   *   *   *   *

That was the beginning of the New Life of
Kashima—the life that Mrs. Boulte made when
her tongue was loosened in the twilight.

Mrs. Vansuythen has never told the Major;
and since he insists upon the maintenance of a
burdensome geniality, she has been compelled to
break her vow of not speaking to Kurrell.
This speech, which must of necessity preserve
the semblance of politeness and interest, serves
admirably to keep alight the flame of jealousy
and dull hatred in Boulte's bosom, as it awakens
the same passions in his wife's heart. Mrs.
Boulte hates Mrs. Vansuythen because she has

taken Ted from her, and in some curious fashion, hates her because Mrs. Vansuythen—and here the wife's eyes see far more clearly than the husband's—detests Ted. And Ted—that gallant captain and honorable man—knows now that it is possible to hate a woman once loved, even to the verge of wishing to silence her forever with blows. Above all, is he shocked that Mrs. Boulte can not see the error of her ways.

Boulte and he go out tiger-shooting together in amity and all good-friendship. Boulte has put their relationship on a most satisfactory footing.

"You're a blackguard," he says to Kurrell, "and I've lost any self-respect I may ever have had; but when you're with me, I can feel certain that you are not with Mrs. Vansuythen, or making Emma miserable."

Kurrell endures anything that Boulte may say to him. Sometimes they are away for three days together, and then the Major insists upon his wife going over to sit with Mrs. Boulte; although Mrs. Vansuythen has repeatedly avowed that she prefers her husband's company to any in the world. From the way in which she clings to him, she would certainly appear to be speaking the truth.

But, of course, as the Major says, "in a little Station we must all be friendly."

THE HILL OF ILLUSION

WHAT rendered vain their deep desire?
A God, a God their severance ruled,
And bade between their shores to be
The unplumbed, salt, estranging sea.
—*M. Arnold.*

HE.—Tell your jhampanis not to hurry so, dear. They forget I'm fresh from the Plains."

SHE.—Sure proof that I have not been going out with any one. Yes, they are an untrained crew. Where do we go?

HE.—As usual—to the world's end. No, Jakko.

SHE.—Have your pony led after you, then. It's a long round.

HE.—And for the last time, thank Heaven!

SHE.—Do you mean *that* still? I didn't dare to write to you about it . . . all these months.

HE.—Mean it! I've been shaping my affairs to that end since Autumn. What makes you speak as though it had occurred to you for the first time?

SHE.—I? Oh! I don't know. I've had long enough to think, too.

HE.—And you've changed your mind?

SHE.—No. You ought to know that I am a

miracle of constancy. What are your—arrangements?

HE.—*Ours*, Sweetheart, please.

SHE.—Ours, be it then. My poor boy, how the prickly heat has marked your forehead! Have you ever tried sulphate of copper in water?

HE.—It'll go away in a day or two up here. The arrangements are simple enough. Tonga in the early morning—reach Kalka at twelve—Umballa at seven—down, straight by night-train, to Bombay, and then the steamer of the 21st for Rome. That's my idea. The Continent and Sweden—a ten-week honeymoon.

SHE.—Ssh! Don't talk of it in that way. It makes me afraid. Guy, how long have we two been insane?

HE.—Seven months and fourteen days; I forget the odd hours exactly, but I'll think.

SHE.—I only wanted to see if you remembered. Who are those two on the Blessington Road?

HE.—Eabrey and the Penner woman. What do they matter to *us?* Tell me everything that you've been doing and saying and thinking.

SHE.—Doing little, saying less, and thinking a great deal. I've hardly been out at all.

HE.—That was wrong of you. You haven't been moping?

SHE.—Not very much. Can you wonder that I'm disinclined for amusement?

He.—Frankly, I do. Where was the difficulty?

She.—In this only. (The more people I know and the more I'm known here, the wider spread will be the news of the crash when it comes. I don't like that.

He.—Nonsense. We shall be out of it.

She.—You think so?

He.—I'm sure of it, if there is any power in steam or horse-flesh to carry us away. Ha! ha!

She.—And the *fun* of the situation comes in —where, my Launcelot?

He.—Nowhere, Guinevere. I was only thinking of something.

She.—They say men have a keener sense of humor than women. Now *I* was thinking of the scandal.

He.—Don't think of anything so ugly. We shall be beyond it.

She.—It will be there all the same—in the mouths of Simla—telegraphed over India, and talked of at the dinners—and when He goes out they will stare at Him to see how He takes it. And we shall be dead, Guy dear—dead and cast into the outer darkness where there is—

He.—Love at least. Isn't that enough?

She.—I have said so.

He.—And you think so still?

She.—What do *you* think?

He.— What have I *done?* It means equal ruin to me, as the world reckons it—outcasting, the loss of my appointment, the breaking off of my life's work. I pay my price.

SHE.—And are you so much above the world that you can afford to pay it? Am I?

HE.—My Divinity—what else?

SHE.—A very ordinary woman, I'm afraid, but, so far, respectable. How do you do, Mrs. Middleditch? Your husband? I think he's riding down to Annandale with Colonel Statters. Yes, isn't it divine after the rain? . . . Guy, how long am I to be allowed to bow to Mrs. Middleditch? Till the 17th?

HE.—Frowsy Scotch woman! What is the use of bringing her into the discussion? You were saying?

SHE.—Nothing. Have you ever seen a man hanged?

HE.—Yes, once.

SHE.—What was it for?

HE.—Murder, of course.

SHE.—Murder. Is that so great a sin after all? I wonder how he felt before the drop fell?

HE.—I don't think he felt much. What a gruesome little woman it is this evening! You're shivering. Put on your cape, dear.

SHE.—I think I will. Oh! look at the mist coming over Sanjaoli; and I thought we should have sunshine on the Ladies' Mile! Let's turn back.

HE.—What's the good? There's a cloud on Elysium Hill, and that means it's foggy all down the Mall. We'll go on. It'll blow away before we get to the Convent, perhaps. Jove! It is chilly.

SHE.—You feel it, fresh from below. Put on your ulster. What do you think of my cape?

HE.—Never ask a man his opinion of a woman's dress when he is desperately and abjectly in love with the wearer. Let me look. Like everything else of yours, it's perfect. Where did you get it from?

SHE.—He gave it me, on Wednesday . . . our wedding-day, you know.

HE.—The deuce He did! He's growing generous in his old age. D'you like all that frilly, bunchy stuff at the throat? I don't.

SHE.—Don't you?

> "Kind Sir, o' your courtesy,
>   As you go by the town, Sir,
> Pray you o' your love for me,
>   Buy me a russet gown, Sir."

HE.—I won't say: "Keek into the draw-well, Janet, Janet." Only wait a little, darling, and you shall be stocked with russet gowns and everything else.

SHE.—And when the frocks wear out, you'll get me new ones . . . and everything else?

HE.—Assuredly.

SHE.—I wonder!

HE.—Look here, Sweetheart, I didn't spend two days and two nights in the train to hear you

wonder. I thought we'd settled all that at Shaifazehat.

SHE (dreamily).—At Shaifazehat? Does the
Station go on still. That was ages and *ages* ago.
It must be crumbling to pieces. All except the
Amirtollah kutcha road. I don't believe *that*
could crumble till the Day of Judgment.

HE.—You think so? What *is* the mood now?

SHE.—I can't tell. How cold it is! Let us get
on quickly.

HE.—Better walk a little. Stop your jhampanis and get out. What's the matter with you
this evening, dear?

SHE.—Nothing. You must grow accustomed
to my ways. If I'm boring you I can go home.
Here's Captain Congleton coming; I dare say
he'll be willing to escort me.

HE.—Goose! Between *us,* too! *Damn* Captain Congleton. There!

SHE.—Chivalrous Knight! Is it your habit
to swear much in talking? It jars a little, and
you might swear at me.

HE.—My angel! I didn't know what I was
saying; and you changed so quickly that I couldn't
follow. I'll apologize in dust and ashes.

SHE.—Spare those. There'll be enough of
them later on. Good-night, Captain Congleton.
Going to the singing-quadrilles already? What
dances am I giving you next week? No! You
must have written them down wrong. Five and
Seven, I said. If you've made a mistake, I cer-

tainly don't intend to suffer for it. You must alter your program.

HE.—I thought you told me that you had not been going out much this season?

SHE.—Quite true, but when I do I dance with Captain Congleton. He dances very nicely.

HE.—And sit out with him, I suppose?

SHE.—Yes. Have you any objections? Shall I stand under the chandelier in future?

HE.—What does he talk to you about?

SHE.—What do men talk about when they sit out?

HE.—Ugh! Don't! Well, now I'm up. You must dispense with the fascinating Congleton for a while. I don't like him.

SHE (after a pause).—Do you know what you have said?

HE.—Can't say that I do, exactly. I'm not in the best of tempers.

SHE.—So I see . . . and feel. My true and faithful lover, where is your "eternal constancy," "unalterable trust," and "reverent devotion?" I remember those phrases; you seem to have forgotten them. I mention a man's name—

HE.—A good deal more than that.

SHE.—Well, speak to him about a dance—perhaps the last dance that I shall ever dance in my life before I . . . before I go away; and you at once distrust and insult me.

HE.—I never said a word.

SHE.—How much did you imply? Guy, is *this* amount of confidence to be our stock to start the new life on?

HE.—No, of course not. I didn't mean that. On my word and honor, I didn't. Let it pass, dear. Please let it pass.

SHE.—This once—yes—and a second time, and again and again, all through the years when I shall be unable to resent it. You want too much, my Launcelot, and . . . you know too much.

HE.—How do you mean?

SHE.—That is a part of the punishment. There *can not* be perfect trust between us.

HE.—In Heaven's name, why not?

SHE.—Hush! The Other Place is quite enough. Ask yourself.

HE.—I don't follow.

SHE.—You trust me so implicitly that when I look at another man . . . Never mind. Guy, have you ever made love to a girl—a *good* girl?

HE.—Something of the sort. Centuries ago —in the Dark Ages, before I ever met you, dear.

SHE.—Tell me what you said to her.

HE.—What does a man say to a girl? I've forgotten.

SHE.—*I* remember. He tells her that he trusts her and worships the ground she walks on, and that he'll love and honor and protect her till her dying day; and so she marries in that belief. At least, I speak of one girl who was *not* protected.

HE.—Well, and then?

SHE.—And then, Guy, and then, that girl needs ten times the love and trust and honor—yes, *honor*—that was enough when she was only a mere wife if—if—the second life she elects to lead is to be made even bearable. Do you understand?

HE.—Even bearable! It'll be Paradise.

SHE.—Ah! Can you give me all I've asked for —not now, nor a few months later, but when you begin to think of what you might have done if you had kept your own appointment and your caste here—when you begin to look upon me as a drag and a burden? I shall want it most then, Guy, for there will be no one in the wide world but you.

HE.—You're a little overtired to-night, Sweetheart, and you're taking a stage view of the situation. After the necessary business in the Courts, the road is clear to—

SHE.—"The holy state of matrimony!" Ha! ha! ha!

HE.—Ssh! Don't laugh in that horrible way!

SHE.—I—I c-c-c-can't help it! Isn't it too absurd! Ah! Ha! ha! ha! Guy, stop me quick, or I shall—l-l-laugh till we get to the Church.

HE.—For goodness' sake, stop! Don't make an exhibition of yourself. What is the matter with you?

SHE.—N-nothing. I'm better now.

HE.—That's all right. One moment, dear.

There's a little whisp of hair got loose from behind your right ear, and it's straggling over your cheek. So!

She.—Thank'oo. I'm 'fraid my hat's on one side, too.

He.—What do you wear these huge dagger bonnet-skewers for? They're big enough to kill a man with.

She.—Oh! Don't kill *me*, though. You're sticking it into my head! Let *me* do it. You men are so clumsy.

He.—Have you had many opportunities of comparing us—in this sort of work?

She.—Guy, what is my name?

He.—Eh! I don't follow.

She.—Here's my card-case. Can you read?

He.—Yes. Well?

She.—Well, that answers your question. You You know the other man's name. Am I sufficiently humbled, or would you like to ask me if there is any one else?

He.—I see now. My darling, I never meant that for an instant. I was only joking. There! Lucky there's no one on the road. They'd be scandalized.

She.—They'll be more scandalized before the end.

He.—Do-on't. I don't like you to talk in that way.

She.—Unreasonable man! Who asked me to face the situation and accept it? Tell me, do I look like Mrs. Penner? *Do* I look like a naughty woman? *Swear* I don't! Give me your word of honor, my *honorable* friend, that I'm not like Mrs. Buzgago. That's the way she stands, with her hands clasped at the back of her head. D'you like that?

HE.—Don't be affected.

SHE.—I'm not. I'm Mrs. Buzgago. Listen!

> "Pendant une anne' toute entiere,
> Le regiment n'a pas r'paru.
> Au Ministere de la Guerre
> On le r'porta comme perdu.

> "On se r'noncait a r'trouver sa trace,
> Quand un matin subitement,
> On le vit r'paraitre sur la place
> L'Colonel toujours en avant."

That's the way she rolls her r's. *Am* I like her?

HE.—No; but I object when you go on like an actress and sing stuff of that kind. Where in the world did you pick up the *Chanson du Colonel?* It isn't a drawing-room song. It isn't proper.

SHE.—Mrs. Buzgago taught it me. She is both drawing-room and proper and in another month she'll shut her drawing-room to me, and, thank God, she isn't as improper as I am. Oh, Guy, Guy! I wish I was like some women, and had no scruples about—what is it Keene says?— "Wearing a corpse's hair, and being false to the bread they eat."

HE.—I am only a man of limited intelligence,

and just now, very bewildered. When you have *quite* finished flashing through all your moods, tell me, and I'll try to understand the last one.

SHE.—Moods, Guy! I haven't any. I'm sixteen years old, and you're just twenty, and you've been waiting for two hours outside the school in the cold. And now I've met you, and now we're walking home together. Does *that* suit you, My Imperial Majesty?

HE.—No. We aren't children. Why can't you be rational?

SHE.—He asks me that when I'm going to commit social suicide for his sake, and, and . . . I don't want to be French and rave about *"ma mère,"* but have I ever told you that I have a mother, and a brother who was my pet before I married? He's married now. Can't you imagine the pleasure that the news of the elopement will give him? Have *you* any people at home, Guy, to be pleased with your performances?

HE.—One or two. We can't make omelets without breaking eggs.

SHE (slowly).—I don't see the necessity—

HE.—Hah! What do you mean?

SHE.—Shall I speak the truth?

HE.—Under the circumstances, perhaps it *would* be as well.

SHE.—Guy, I'm afraid.

HE.—I thought we'd settled all that. What of?

SHE.—Of you.

He.—Oh, damn it all! The old business! This is *too* bad!

She.—Of *you*.

He.—And what now?

She.—What do you think of me?

He.—Beside the question altogether. What do you intend to do?

She.—I daren't risk it. I'm afraid. If I could only cheat . . .

He.—*A la* Buzgago? No, *thanks*. That's the one point on which I have any notion of Honor. I won't eat his salt and steal too. I'll loot openly or not at all.

She.—I never meant anything else.

He.—Then, why in the world do you pretend not to be willing to come?

She.—It's *not* pretense, Guy. I *am* afraid.

He.—Please explain.

She.—It can't last, Guy. It can't last. You'll get angry, and then you'll swear, and then you'll get jealous, and then you'll mistrust me—you do *now*—and you yourself will be the best reason for doubting. And I—what shall I do? I shall be no better than Mrs. Buzgago found out—no better than any one. And you'll *know* that. Oh, Guy, can't you *see?*

He.—I see that you are desperately unreasonable, little woman.

She.—There! The moment I begin to object, you get angry. What will you do when I am only your property—stolen property? It can't be,

Guy— It can't be! I thought it could, but it *can't*. You'll get tired of me.

HE.—I tell you I shall *not*. Won't anything make you understand that?

SHE.—There, can't you see? If you speak to me like that now, you'll call me horrible names later, if I don't do everything as you like. And if you were cruel to me, Guy, where should I go —where should I go? I can't trust you!

HE.—I suppose I ought to say that I *can* trust you. I've ample reason.

SHE.—*Please* don't, dear. It hurts as much as if you hit me.

HE.—It isn't exactly pleasant for me.

SHE.—I can't help it. I wish I were dead! I can't trust you, and I don't trust myself. Oh, Guy, let it die away and be forgotten!

HE.—Too late now. I don't understand you —I won't—and I can't trust myself to talk this evening. May I call to-morrow?

SHE.—Yes. *No!* Oh, give me time! The day after. I get into my 'rickshaw here and meet Him at Peliti's. You ride.

HE.—I'll go on to Peliti's, too. I think I want a drink. My world's knocked about my ears, and the stars are falling. Who are those brutes howling in the Old Library?

SHE.—They're rehearsing the singing-quad-rilles for the Fancy Ball. Can't you hear Mrs. Buzgago's voice? She has a solo. It's quite a new idea. Listen!

Mrs. Buzgago (in the Old Library, *con. molt. exp.*).

> "See-saw! Margery Daw!
>   Sold her bed to lie upon straw.
> Wasn't she a silly slut
>   To sell her bed and die upon dirt?"

Captain Congleton, I'm going to alter that to "flirt." It sounds better.

He.—No, I've changed my mind about the drink. Good-night, little lady. I shall see you to-morrow.

She.—Ye-es. Good-night, Guy. *Don't* be angry with me.

He.—Angry! You *know* I trust you absolutely. Good-night, and—God bless you!

(Three seconds later. *Solus.*) H'm! I'd give something to discover whether there's another man at the back of all this.

A SECOND-RATE WOMAN

Est fuga, volvitur rota,
  On we drift: where looms the dim port?
One Two Three Four Five contribute their quota
  Something is gained if one caught but the import,
Show it us, Hugues of Saxe-Gotha.
                    —*Master Hugues of Saxe-Gotha.*

"Dressed! Don't tell me that woman ever dressed in her life. She stood in the middle of the room while her ayah—no, her husband—it it *must* have been a man—threw her clothes at her. She then did her hair with her fingers, and rubbed her bonnet in the flue under the bed. I *know* she did, as well as if I had assisted at the orgy. Who is she?" said Mrs. Hauksbee.

"Don't!" said Mrs. Mallowe, feebly. "You make my head ache. I'm miserable to-day. Stay me with *fondants,* comfort me with chocolates, for I am . . . Did you bring anything from Peliti's?"

"Questions to begin with. You shall have the sweets when you have answered them. Who and what is the creature? There were at least a half dozen men round her, and she appeared to be going to sleep in their midst.

"Delville," said Mrs. Mallowe, " 'Shady' Del-

ville, to distinguish her from Mrs. Jim of that
ilk. She dances as untidily as she dresses, I believe, and her husband is somewhere in Madras.
Go and call, if you are interested."

"What have I to do with Shigramitish
women? She merely caught my attention for a
minute, and I wondered at the attraction that a
dowd has for a certain type of man. I expected
to see her walk out of her clothes—until I looked
at her eyes."

"Hooks and eyes, surely," drawled Mrs. Mallowe.

"Don't be clever, Polly. You make my head
ache. And round this hayrick stood a crowd of
men—a positive crowd!"

"Perhaps *they* also expected—"

"Polly, don't be Rabelaisian!"

Mrs. Mallowe curled herself up comfortably
on the sofa, and turned her attention to the
sweets. She and Mrs. Hauksbee shared the same
house at Simla; and these things befell two seasons after the matter of Otis Yeere, which has
been already recorded.

Mrs. Hauksbee stepped into the veranda and
looked down upon the Mall, her forehead puck-
ered with thought.

"Hah!" said Mrs. Hauksbee, shortly. "Indeed!"

"What is it?" said Mrs. Mallowe, sleepily.

"That dowd and The Dancing Master—to
whom I object."

"Why to The Dancing Master? He is a middle-aged gentleman, of reprobate and romantic tendencies, and tries to be a friend of mine."

"Then make up your mind to lose him. Dowds cling by nature, and I should imagine that this animal—how terrible her bonnet looks from above!—is specially clingsome."

"She is welcome to The Dancing Master so far as I am concerned. I never could take an interest in a monotonous liar. The frustrated aim of his life is to persuade people that he is a bachelor."

"O-oh! I think I've met that sort of man before. And isn't he?"

"No. He confided that to me a few days ago. Ugh! Some men ought to be killed."

"What happened then?"

"He posed as the horror of horrors—a misunderstood man. Heaven knows the *femme incomprise* is sad enough and bad enough—but the other thing!"

"And so fat, too! *I* should have laughed in his face. Men seldom confide in me. How is it they come to you?"

"For the sake of impressing me with their careers in the past. Protect me from men with confidences!"

"And yet you encourage them?"

"What can I do? They talk, I listen, and they vow that I am sympathetic. I know I always pro-

fess astonishment even when the plot is—of the
most old possible."

"Yes. Men are so unblushingly explicit if they
are once allowed to talk, whereas women's confidences are full of reservations and fibs, except—"

"When they go mad and babble of the Unut-
terabilities after a week's acquaintance. Even
then, they always paint thmselves *á la* Mrs.
Gummidge—throwing cold water on *him*. Really,
if you come to consider, we know a great deal
more of men than of our own sex."

"And the extraordinary thing is that men will
never believe it. They say we are trying to hide
something."

"They are generally doing that on their own
account—and very clumsily they hide. Alas!
These chocolates pall upon me, and I haven't
eaten more than a dozen. I think I shall go to
sleep."

"Then you'll get fat, dear. If you took more
exercise and a more intelligent interest in your
neighbors, you would—"

"Be as universally loved as Mrs. Hauksbee.
You're a darling in many ways, and I like you—
you are not a woman's woman—but *why* do you
trouble yourself about mere human beings?"

"Because, in the absence of angels, who, I am
sure, would be horribly dull, men and women are
the most fascinating things in the whole wide
world, lazy one. I am interested in The Dowd—
I am interested in The Dancing Master—I am

interested in the Hawley Boy—and I am interested in *you*.

"Why couple *me* with the Hawley Boy? He is your property."

"Yes, and in his own guileless speech, I'm making a good thing out of him. When he is slightly more reformed, and has passed his Higher Standard, or whatever the authorities think fit to exact from him, I shall select a pretty little girl, the Holt girl, I think, and"—here she waved her hands airily—" 'whom Mrs. Hauksbee hath joined together let no man put asounder.' That's all."

"And when you have yoked May Holt with the most notorious detrimental in Simla, and earned the undying hatred of Mamma Holt, what will you do with me, Dispenser of the Destinies of the Universe?"

Mrs. Hauksbee dropped into a low chair in front of the fire, and, chin in hand, gazed long and steadfastly at Mrs. Mallowe.

"I do not know," she said, shaking her head, *"what* I shall do with you, dear. It's obviously impossible to marry you to some one else—your husband would object, and the experiment might not be successful after all. I think I shall begin by preventing you from—what is it?—'sleeping on ale-house benches and snoring in the sun.' "

"Don't. I don't like your quotations. They are so rude. Go to the Library and bring me new books."

"While you sleep? *No!* If you don't come with me, I shall spread your newest frock on my 'rickshaw-bow, and when any one asks me what I am doing, I shall say that I am going to Phelps's to get it let out. I shall take care that Mrs. Mc-Namara sees me. Put your things on, there's a good girl."

Mrs. Mallowe groaned and obeyed, and the two went off to the Library, where they found Mrs. Delville and the man who went by the nickname of The Dancing Master. By that time Mrs. Mallowe was awake and eloquent.

"That is the Creature!" said Mrs. Hauksbee, with the air of one pointing out a slug in the road.

"No," said Mrs. Mallowe. "The man is the creature. Ugh! Good-evening, Mr. Bent. I thought you were coming to tea this evening."

"Surely it was for to-morrow, was it not?" answered The Dancing Master. "I understood . . . I fancied . . . I'm so sorry. . . . How very unfortunate! . . ."

But Mrs. Mallowe had passed on.

"For the practiced equivocator you said he was," murmured Mrs. Hauksbee, "he strikes *me* as a failure. Now, wherefore should he have preferred a walk with The Dowd to tea with us? Elective affinities, I suppose—both grubby. Polly, I'd never forgive that woman as long as the world rolls."

"I forgive every woman everything," said Mrs. Mallowe. "He will be a sufficient punishment for her.　What a common voice she has!"

Mrs. Delville's voice was not pretty, her carriage was even less lovely, and her raiment was strikingly neglected.　All these facts Mrs. Mallowe absorbed over the top of a magazine.

"Now, *what* is there in her?" said Mrs. Hauksbee.　"Do you see what I meant about the clothes falling off?　If I were a man I would perish sooner than be seen with that rag-bag.　And yet, she has good eyes, but—oh!"

"What is it?"

"She doesn't know how to use them!　On my Honor, she does not.　Look!　Oh, look!　Untidiness I can endure, but ignorance never!　The woman's a fool."

"H'sh!　She'll hear you."

"All the women in Simla are fools.　She'll think I mean some one else.　Now she's going out.　What a thoroughly objectionable couple she and The Dancing Master make!　Which reminds me.　Do you suppose they'll ever dance together?"

"Wait and see.　I don't envy her conversation of The Dancing Master—loathly man!　His wife ought to be up here before long?"

"Do you know anything about him?"

"Only what he told me.　It may be all a fiction. He married a girl bred in the country, I think, and, being an honorable, chivalrous soul, told me that he repented his bargain, and sent her to her mother as often as possible—a person who has lived in the Doon since the memory of man, and goes to Mussoorie when other people go home. The wife is with her at present. So he says."

"Babies?"

"One only, but he talks of his wife in a revolting way. I hated him for it. *He* thought he was being epigrammatic and brilliant."

"That is a vice peculiar to men. I dislike him because he is generally in the wake of some girl, to the disgust of the Eligibles. He will persecute May Holt no more, unless I am much mistaken."

"No. I think Mrs. Delville may occupy his attention for awhile."

"Do you suppose she knows that he is the head of a family?"

"Not from his lips. He swore to me eternal secrecy. Wherefore I tell you. Don't you know that type of man?"

"Not intimately, thank goodness! As a general rule, when a man begins to abuse his wife to me, I find that the Lord gives me wherewith to answer him according to his folly, and we part with a coolness between us. I laugh."

"I'm different. I've no sense of humor."

"Cultivate it, then. It has been my mainstay for more years than I care to think about. A well-educated sense of Humor will save a woman when Religion, Training, and Home influences fail. And we may all need salvation sometimes."

"Do you suppose that the Delville woman has humor?"

"Her dress betrays her. How can a Thing

who wears her *supplément* under her left arm
have any notion of the fitness of things—much
less their folly? If she discards The Dancing
Master after having once seen him dance, I may
respect her. Otherwise—"

"But are we not both assuming a great deal too
much, dear? You saw the woman at Peliti's—
half an hour later you saw her walking with The
Dancing Master—an hour later you met her here
at the Library."

"Still with The Dancing Master, remember."

"Still with The Dancing Master, I admit, but
why on the strength of that should you
imagine—"

"I imagine nothing. I have no imagination. I
am only convinced that The Dancing Master is
attracted to The Dowd because he is objectionable in every way and she in every other. If I
know the man as you have described him, he holds
his wife in deadly subjection at present."

"She is twenty years younger than he."

"Poor wretch! And, in the end, after he has
posed and swaggered and lied—he has a mouth
under that ragged mustache simply made for lies
—he will be rewarded according to his merits."

"I wonder what those really are," said Mrs.
Mallowe.

But Mrs. Hauksbee, her face close to the shelf
of the new books, was humming softly: "What
shall he have who killed the Deer?" She was a
lady of unfettered speech. One month later, she

announced her intention of calling upon Mrs. Delville. Both Mrs. Hauksbee and Mrs. Mallowe were in morning wrappers, and there was great peace in the land.

"I should go as I was," said Mrs. Mallowe. "It would be a delicate compliment to her style."

Mrs. Hauksbee studied herself in the glass.

"Assuming for a moment that she ever darkened these doors, I should put on this robe, after all the others, to show her what a morning-wrapper ought to be. It might enliven her. As it is, I shall go in the dove-colored—sweet emblem of youth and innocence—and shall put on my new gloves."

"If you really are going, dirty tan would be too good; and you know that dove-color spots with the rain."

"I care not. I may make her envious. At least I shall try, though one can not expect very much from a woman who puts a lace tucker into her habit."

"Just Heavens! When did she do that?"

"Yesterday—riding with The Dancing Master. I met them at the back of Jakko, and the rain had made the lace lie down. To complete the effect, she was wearing an unclean terai with the elastic under her chin. I felt almost too well content to take the trouble to despise her."

"The Hawley Boy was riding with you. What did he think?"

"Does a boy ever notice these things? Should

I like him if he did? He stared in the rudest
way, and just when I thought he had seen the
elastic, he said: 'There's something very taking
about that face.' I rebuked him on the spot. I
don't approve of boys being taken by faces."

"Other than your own. I shouldn't be in the
least surprised if the Hawley Boy immediately
went to call."

"I forbid him. Let her be satisfied with The
Dancing Master, and his wife when she comes
up. I'm rather curious to see Mrs. Bent and the
Delville woman together."

Mrs. Hauksbee departed, and at the end of an
hour returned slightly flushed.

"There is no limit to the treachery of youth! I
ordered the Hawley Boy, as he valued my patron-
age, not to call. The first person I stumble over
—literally stumble over—in her poky, dark little
drawing-room is, of course, the Hawley Boy. She
kept us waiting ten minutes, and then emerged as
though she had been tipped out of the dirty-
clothes-basket. You know my way, dear, when I
am at all put out. I was Superior, *c-r-r-r-rush-
ingly* Superior! 'Lifted my eyes to Heaven, and
had heard of nothing—'dropped my eyes on the
carpet, and 'really didn't know'—played with my
card-case and 'supposed so.' The Hawley Boy
giggled like a girl, and I had to freeze him with
scowls between the sentences."

"And she?"

"She sat in a heap on the edge of a couch, and

managed to convey the impression that she was suffering from stomach ache, at the very least. It was all I could do not to ask after her symptoms. When I rose, she grunted just like a buffalo in the water—too lazy to move."

"Are you certain—"

"Am I blind, Polly? Laziness, sheer laziness, nothing else—or her garments were only constructed for sitting down in. I stayed for a quarter of an hour trying to penetrate the gloom, to guess what her surroundings were like, while she stuck out her tongue."

"Lu—*cy!*"

"Well—I'll withdraw the tongue, though I'm sure if she didn't do it when I was in the room, she did the minute I was outside. At any rate, she lay in a lump and grunted. Ask the Hawley Boy, dear. I believe the grunts were meant for sentences, but she spoke so indistinctly that I can't swear to it."

"You are incorrigible, simply."

"I am *not!* Treat me civilly, give me peace with honor, don't put the only available seat facing the window, and a child may eat jam in my lap before Church. But I resent being grunted at. Wouldn't you? Do you suppose that she communicates her views on life and love to The Dancing Master in a set of modulated 'Grmphs'?"

"You attach too much importance to The Dancing Master."

"He came as we went, and The Dowd grew

almost cordial at the sight of him. He smiled
greasily, and moved about that darkened dog-ken-
nel in a suspiciously familiar way."

"Don't be uncharitable. Any sin but that I'll
forgive."

"Listen to the voice of History. I am only de-
scribing what I saw. He entered, the heap on
the sofa revived slightly, and the Hawley Boy
and I came away together. *He* is disillusioned,
but I felt it my duty to lecture him severely for
going there. And that's all."

"Now for pity's sake, leave the wretched creature and The Dancing Master alone. They never
did you any harm."

"No harm. To dress as an example and a
stumbling-block for half Simla, and then to find
this Person who is dressed by the hand of God—
not that I wish to disparage *Him* for a moment,
but you know the tikka-dhurzie way. He attires
those lilies of the field—this Person draws the
eyes of men—and some of them nice men! It's almost enough to make one discard clothing. I
told the Hawley Boy so."

"And what did that sweet youth do?"

"Turned shell-pink and looked across the far
blue hills like a distressed cherub. *Am* I talking
wildly, Polly? Let me say my say, and I shall
be calm. Otherwise I may go abroad and disturb
Simla with a few original reflections. Excepting always your own sweet self, there isn't a

single woman in the land who understands me
when I am—what's the word?"

"*Tête-fêlée,*" suggested Mrs. Mallowe.

"Exactly! And now let us have tiffin. The
demands of Society are exhausting, and as Mrs.
Delville says—" Here Mrs. Hauksbee, to the
horror of the khitmatgars, lapsed into a series of
grunts, while Mrs. Mallowe stared in lazy surprise.

" 'God gie us a gude conceit of oorselves,' "
said Mrs. Hauksbee, piously, returning to her natural speech. "Now, in any other woman that
would have been vulgar. I am consumed with
curiosity to see Mrs. Bent. I expect complications."

"Woman of one idea," said Mrs. Mallowe,
shortly, "all complications are as old as the hills!
I have lived through or near all—*all*—ALL!"

"And yet do not understand that men and
women never behave twice alike. I am old who
was young—if ever I put my head in your lap,
you dear, big skeptic, you will learn that my part-
ing is gauze—but never, no never, have I lost
my interest in men and women. Polly, I shall
see this business out to the bitter end."

"I am going to sleep," said Mrs. Mallowe,
calmly. "I never interfere with men or women
unless I am compelled," and she retired with dig-
nity to her own room.

Mrs. Hauksbee's curiosity was not long left
ungratified, for Mrs. Bent came up to Simla a

few days after the conversation faithfully reported above, and pervaded the Mall by her husband's side.

"Behold!" said Mrs. Hauksbee, thoughtfully
rubbing her nose. "That is the last link of the
chain, if we omit the husband of the Delville,
whoever he may be. Let me consider. The Bents
and the Delvilles inhabit the same hotel; and the
Delville is detested by the Waddy—do you know
the Waddy?—who is almost as big a dowd. The
Waddy also abominates the male Bent, for which,
if her other sins do not weigh too heavily, she will
eventually be caught up to Heaven."

"Don't be irreverent," said Mrs. Mallowe. "I
like Mrs. Bent's face."

"I am discussing the Waddy," returned Mrs.
Hauksbee, loftily. "The Waddy will take the
female Bent apart, after having borrowed—yes!
—everything that she can, from hairpins to
babies' bottles. Such, my dear, is life in a hotel.
The Waddy will tell the female Bent facts and
fictions about The Dancing Master and The
Dowd."

"Lucy, I should like you better if you were
not always looking into people's back bedrooms."

"Anybody can look into their front drawing-
rooms; and remember whatever I do, and whatever I look, I never talk—as the Waddy will. Let
us hope that The Dancing Master's greasy smile
and manner of the pedagogue will 'soften the
heart of that cow,' his wife. If mouths speak

truth, I should think that little Mrs. Bent could get very angry on occasion."

"But what reason has she for being angry?"

"What reason! The Dancing Master in himself is a reason. How does it go? 'If in his life some trivial errors fall, Look in his face and you'll believe them all.' I am prepared to credit any evil of The Dancing Master, because I hate him so. And The Dowd is so disgustingly badly dressed—"

"That she, too, is capable of every iniquity? I always prefer to believe the best of everybody. It saves so much trouble."

"Very good. I prefer to believe the worst. It save useless expenditure of sympathy. And you may be quite certain that the Waddy believes with me."

Mrs. Mallowe sighed and made no answer.

The conversation was held after dinner while Mrs. Hauksbee was dressing for a dance.

"I am too tired to go," pleaded Mrs. Mallowe; and Mrs. Hauksbee left her in peace till two in the morning, when she was aware of emphatic knocking at her door.

"Don't be *very* angry, dear," said Mrs. Hauksbee. "My idiot of an ayah has gone home, and, as I hope to sleep to-night, there isn't a soul in the place to unlace me."

"Oh, this is too bad!" said Mrs. Mallowe, sulkily.

"Can't help it. I'm a lone, lorn grass-widow,

but I will *not* sleep in my stays. And such news, too! Oh, *do* unlace me, there's a darling! The Dowd—The Dancing Master—I and the Hawley Boy— You know the North veranda?"

"How can I do anything if you spin round like this?" protested Mrs. Mallowe, fumbling with the knot of the lace.

"Oh, I forget. I must tell my tale without the aid of your eyes. Do you know you've lovely eyes, dear? Well, to begin with, I took the Hawley Boy to a kala juggah."

"Did he want much taking?"

"Lots! There was an arrangement of loose-boxes in kanats, and *she* was in the next one talking to *him*."

"Which? How? Explain."

"You know what I mean—The Dowd and The Dancing Master. We could hear every word, and we listened shamelessly—'specially the Hawley Boy. Polly, I quite love that woman!"

"This is interesting. There! Now turn round. What happened?"

"One moment. Ah—h! Blessed relief. I've been looking forward to taking them off for the last half hour—which is ominous at my time of life. But, as I was saying, we listened and heard The Dowd drawl worse than ever. She drops her final g's like a barmaid or a blue-blooded Aide-de-Camp. 'Look he'ere, you're gettin' too fond o' me," she said, and The Dancing Master owned it was so in language that nearly made me

ill. The Dowd reflected for awhile. Then we
heard her say, 'Look he'ere, Mister Bent, why
are you such an aw-ful liar?' I nearly exploded
while The Dancing Master denied the charge. It
seems he never told her he was a married man."

"I said he wouldn't."

"And she had taken this to heart, on personal
grounds, I suppose. She drawled along for five
minutes, reproaching him with his perfidy, and
grew quite motherly. 'Now you've got a nice
little wife of your own—you have,' she said.
'She's ten times too good for a fat old man like
you, and, look he'ere, you never told me a word
about her, and I've been thinkin' about it a good
deal, and I think you're a liar.' Wasn't that de-
licious? The Dancing Master maundered and
raved till the Hawley Boy suggested that he
should burst in and beat him. His voice runs up
into an impassioned squeak when he is afraid.
The Dowd must be an extraordinary woman.
She explained that had he been a bachelor she
might not have objected to his devotion; but since
he was a married man and the father of a very
nice baby, she considered him a hypocrite, and
this she repeated twice. She wound up her drawl
with: 'An' I'm tellin' you this because your wife
is angry with me, an' I hate quarrelin' with any
other woman, an' I like your wife. You know
how you have behaved for the last six weeks.
You shouldn't have done it, indeed you shouldn't.
You're too old an' too fat.' Can't you imagine

how The Dancing Master would wince at that! 'Now go away,' she said. 'I don't want to tell you what I think of you, because I think you are not nice. I'll stay he'ere till the next dance begins.' Did you think that the creature had so much in her?"

"I never studied her as closely as you did. It sounds unnatural. What happened?"

"The Dancing Master attempted blandishment, reproof, jocularity, and the style of the Lord High Warden, and I had almost to pinch the Hawley.Boy to make him keep quiet. She grunted at the end of each sentence, and, in the end, *he* went away swearing to himself, quite like a man in a novel. He looked more objectionable than ever. I laughed. I love that woman—in spite of her clothes. And now I'm going to bed. What do you think of it?"

"I shan't begin to think till the morning," said Mrs. Mallowe, yawning. "Perhaps she spoke the truth. They do fly into it by accident sometimes."

Mrs. Hauksbee's account of her eavesdropping was an ornate one, but truthful in the main. For reasons best known to herself, Mrs. "Shady" Delville had turned upon Mr. Bent and rent him limb from limb, casting him away limp and disconcerted ere she withdrew the light of her eyes from him permanently. Being a man of resource, and anything but pleased in that he had been called both old and fat, he gave Mrs. Bent to un-

derstand that he had, during her absence in the
Doon, been the victim of unceasing persecution
at the hands of Mrs. Delville, and he told the tale
so often and with such eloquence that he ended in
believing it, while his wife marveled at the manners and customs of "some women." When the
situation showed signs of languishing, Mrs.
Waddy was always on hand to wake the smolder-
ing fires of suspicion in Mrs. Bent's bosom, and
to contribute generally to the peace and comfort
of the hotel. Mr. Bent's life was not a happy
one, for if Mrs. Waddy's story were true, he was,
argued his wife, untrustworthy to the last degree. If his own statement was true, his charms
of manner and conversation were so great that
he needed constant surveillance. And he received
it, till he repented genuinely of his marriage and
neglected his personal appearance. Mrs. Delville
alone in the hotel was unchanged. She removed
her chair some six paces toward the head of the
table, and occasionally in the twilight ventured
on timid overtures of friendship to Mrs. Bent,
which were repulsed.

"She does it for my sake," hinted the virtuous
Bent.

"A dangerous and designing woman," purred
Mrs. Waddy.

Worst of all, every other hotel in Simla was
full!

     *　　*　　*　　*　　*　　*

"Polly, are you afraid of diphtheria?"

"Of nothing in the world except smallpox. Diphtheria kills, but it doesn't disfigure. Why do you ask?"

"Because the Bent baby has got it, and the whole hotel is upside down in consequence. The Waddy has 'set her five young on the rail' and fled. The Dancing Master fears for his precious throat, and that miserable little woman, his wife, has no notion of what ought to be done. She wanted to put it into a mustard bath—for croup!"

"Where did you learn all this?"

"Just now, on the Mall. Dr. Howlen told me. The Manager of the hotel is abusing the Bents, and the Bents are abusing the Manager. They *are* a feckless couple."

"Well. What's on your mind?"

"This; and I know it's a grave thing to ask. Would you seriously object to my bringing the child over here, with its mother?"

"On the most strict understanding that we see nothing of the Dancing Master."

"He will be only too glad to stay away. Polly, you're an angel. The woman really is at her wits' end."

"And you know nothing about her, careless, and would hold her up to public scorn if it gave you a minute's amusement. Therefore you risk your life for the sake of her brat. No, Loo, *I'm* not the angel. I shall keep to my rooms and avoid her. But do as you please—only tell me why you do it."

Mrs. Hauksbee's eyes softened; she looked out of the window and back into Mrs. Mallowe's face.

"I don't know," said Mrs. Hauksbee, simply.

"You dear!"

"Polly!—and for aught you knew you might have taken my fringe off. Never do that again without warning. Now we'll get the rooms ready. I don't suppose I shall be allowed to circulate in society for a month."

"And I also. Thank goodness I shall at last get all the sleep I want."

Much to Mrs. Bent's surprise, she and the baby were brought over to the house almost before she knew where she was. Bent was devoutly and undisguisedly thankful, for he was afraid of the infection, and also hoped that a few weeks in the hotel alone with Mrs. Delville might lead to some sort of explanation.

Mrs. Bent had cast her jealousy to the winds in her fear for her child's life.

"We can give you good milk," said Mrs. Hauksbee to her, "and our house is much nearer to the Doctor's than the hotel, and you won't feel as though you were living in a hostile camp. Where is the dear Mrs. Waddy? She seems to be a particular friend of yours."

"They've all left me," said Mrs. Bent, bitterly. "Mrs. Waddy went first. She said I ought to be

ashamed of myself for introducing diseases
there, and I am *sure* it wasn't my fault that little
Dora—"

"How nice!" cooed Mrs. Hauksbee. "The
Waddy is an infectious disease herself—'more
quickly caught than the plague, and the taker
runs presently mad.' I lived next door to her at
the Elysium, three years ago. Now, see, you
won't give us the *least* trouble, and I've orna-
mented all the house with sheets soaked in carbolic. It smells comforting, doesn't it? Remember I'm always in call, and my ayah's at your
service when yours goes to her meals, and . . .
and . . . if you cry I'll *never* forgive you."

Dora Bent occupied her mother's unprofitable
attention through the day and the night. The
Doctor called thrice in the twenty-four hours, and
the house reeked with the smell of the Condy's
Fluid, chlorine water, and carbolic acid washes.
Mrs. Mallowe kept to her own rooms—she considered that she had made sufficient concessions in the
cause of humanity—and Mrs. Hauksbee was
more esteemed by the Doctor as a help in the sick-
room than the half-distraught mother.

"I know nothing of illness," said Mrs. Hauksbee to the Doctor. "Only tell me what to do, and
I'll do it."

"Keep that crazy woman from kissing the
child, and let her have as little to do with the
nursing as you possibly can," said the Doctor;
"I'd turn her out of the sick-room, but that I

honestly believe she'd die of anxiety. She is less
than no good, and I depend on you and the ayahs,
remember."

Mrs. Hauksbee accepted the responsibility,
even though it painted olive hollows under her
eyes and forced her into her oldest dresses. Mrs.
Bent clung to her with more than child-like faith.

"I *know* you'll make Dora well, won't you?"
she said at least twenty times a day; and twenty
times a day Mrs. Hauksbee answered valiantly:
"Of course I will."

But Dora did not improve, and the Doctor
seemed to be always in the house.

"There's some danger of the thing taking a
bad turn," he said; "I'll come over between three
and four in the morning to-morrow."

"Good gracious!" said Mrs. Hauksbee. "He
never told me what the turn would be! My education has been horribly neglected; and I have
only this foolish mother-woman to fall back
upon."

The night wore through slowly, and Mrs.
Hauksbee dozed in a chair by the fire. There
was a dance at the Viceregal Lodge, and she
dreamed of it till she was aware of Mrs. Bent's
anxious eyes staring into her own.

"Wake up! Wake up! Do something!" cried
Mrs. Bent, piteously. "Dora's choking to death!
Do you mean to let her die?"

Mrs. Hauksbee jumped to her feet and bent
over the bed. The child was fighting for breath.

while the mother wrung her hands in despair.

"Oh, what can I do? What can I do? She won't stay still! I can't hold her. Why didn't the Doctor say this was coming?" screamed Mrs. Bent. *"Won't* you help me? She's dying!"

"I—I've never seen a child die before!" stammered Mrs. Hauksbee, feebly, and then—let no one blame her weakness after the strain of long watching—she broke down, and covered her face with her hands. The ayahs on the threshold snored peacefully.

There was a rattle of 'rickshaw wheels below, the clash of an opening door, a heavy step on the stairs, and Mrs. Delville entered to find Mrs. Bent screaming for the Doctor as she ran round the room. Mrs. Hauksbee, her hands to her ears, and her face buried in the chintz of a chair, was quivering with pain at each cry from the bed, and murmuring: "Thank God, I never bore a child! Oh! thank God, I never bore a child!"

Mrs. Delville looked at the bed for an instant, took Mrs. Bent by the shoulders, and said quietly: "Get me some caustic. Be quick."

The mother obeyed mechanically. Mrs. Delville had thrown herself down by the side of the child and was opening its mouth.

"Oh, you're killing her!" cried Mrs. Bent. "Where's the Doctor? Leave her alone!"

Mrs. Delville made no reply for a minute, but busied herself with the child.

"Now the caustic, and hold a lamp behind my

shoulder. *Will* you do as you are told? The acid-bottle, if you don't know what I mean," she said.

A second time Mrs. Delville bent over the child. Mrs. Hauksbee, her face still hidden, sobbed and shivered. One of the ayahs staggered sleepily into the room, yawning: "Doctor Sahib hai."

Mrs. Delville turned her head.

"You're only just in time," she said. "It was chokin' her when I came, an' I've burnt it."

"There was no sign of the membrane getting to the air-passages after the last steaming. It was the general weakness, I feared," said the Doctor, half to himself, and he whispered as he looked: "You've done what I should have been afraid to do without consultation."

"She was dyin'," said Mrs. Delville, under her breath. "Can you do anythin'? What a mercy it was I went to the dance!"

Mrs. Hauksbee raised her head.

"Is it all over?" she gasped. "I'm useless. I'm worse than useless! What are you doing here?"

She stared at Mrs. Delville, and Mrs. Bent, realizing for the first time who was the Goddess from the Machine, stared also.

Then Mrs. Delville made explanation, putting on a dirty long glove and smoothing a crumpled and ill-fitting ball-dress.

"I was at the dance, an' the Doctor was tellin'

me about your baby bein' so ill. So I came away early, an' your door was open, an' I—I lost my boy this way six months ago, an' I've been tryin' to forget it ever since, an' I—I—I am very sorry for intrudin' an' anythin' that has happened."

Mrs. Bent was putting out the Doctor's eye with a lamp as he stooped over Dora.

"Take it away," said the Doctor. "I think the child will do, thanks to you, Mrs. Delville. *I* should have come too late, but, I assure you"— he was addressing himself to Mrs. Delville—"I had not the faintest reason to expect *this*. The membrane must have grown like a mushroom. Will one of you ladies help me, please?"

He had reason for his concluding sentence. Mrs. Hauksbee had thrown herself into Mrs. Delville's arms, where she was weeping copiously, and Mrs. Bent was unpicturesquely mixed up with both, while from the triple triangle came the sound of many sobs and much promiscuous kissing.

"Good gracious! I've spoiled all your beautiful roses!" said Mrs. Hauksbee, lifting her head from the lump of crushed gum and calico atrocities on Mrs. Delville's shoulder and hurrying to the Doctor.

Mrs. Delville picked up her shawl, and slouched out of the room, mopping her eyes with the glove that she had not put on.

"I always said she was more than a woman,"

sobbed Mrs. Hauksbee, hysterically, "and that proves it!"

* * * * * *

Six weeks later, Mrs. Bent and Dora had returned to the hotel. Mrs. Hauksbee had come out of the Valley of Humiliation, had ceased to reproach herself for her collapse in an hour of bitter need, and was even beginning to direct the affairs of the world as before.

"So nobody died, and everything went off as it should, and I kissed The Dowd. Polly, I feel so old. Does it show in my face?"

"Kisses don't, as a rule, do they? Of course you know what the result of The Dowd's providential arrival has been."

"They ought to build her a statue—only no sculptor dare reproduce those skirts."

"Ah!" said Mrs. Mallowe, quietly. "She has found another reward. The Dancing Master has been smirking through Simla, giving every one to understand that she came because of her undying love for him—for him—to save *his* child, and all Simla naturally believes this."

"But Mrs. Bent——"

"Mrs. Bent believes it more than any one else. She won't speak to The Dowd now. *Isn't* The Dancing Master an angel?"

Mrs. Hauksbee lifted up her voice and raged

till bedtime. The doors of the two rooms stood open.

"Polly," said a voice from the darkness, "what did that American-heiress-globe-trotter girl say last season when she was tipped out of her 'rickshaw turning a corner? Some absurd adjective that made the man who picked her up explode.

"'Paltry,'" said Mrs. Mallowe. "Through her nose—like this—'Ha-ow pahltry!'"

"Exactly," said the voice. "Ha-ow pahltry it all is!"

"Which?"

"Everything. Babies, Diphtheria, Mrs. Bent and the Dancing Master, I whooping in a chair, and The Dowd dropping in from the clouds. I wonder what the motive was—*all* the motives."

"Um!"

"What do *you* think?"

"Don't ask me. She was a woman. Go to sleep."

THE END